Weekly Reader

Children's Book Club

EDUCATION CENTER • COLUMBUS 16, OHIO

Presents

A DOG *for* DAVIE'S HILL

by

CLARE BICE

A 1957 Selection of the
WEEKLY READER

Children's Book Club

EDUCATION CENTER, COLUMBUS 16, OHIO

A DOG for DAVIE'S HILL

WRITTEN AND ILLUSTRATED

BY CLARE BICE

—

The Macmillan Company, New York

WEEKLY READER

Children's Book Club

Edition, 1957

PRINTED IN THE UNITED STATES OF AMERICA
AMERICAN BOOK–STRATFORD PRESS, INC., NEW YORK

To my Mother and her clan, the McKays and McLeods, to Megan and Kevin, and to the good Highland people who were our hosts and our friends.

Special Notice to Book Club Members

★ This book is a selection of the WEEKLY READER CHILDREN'S BOOK CLUB. It was chosen especially for our members by the Weekly Reader Selection Board after careful consideration of hundreds of other books for girls and boys.

Members of the WEEKLY READER CHILDREN'S BOOK CLUB receive six or more exciting books during the year — including one or more Free Bonus Books upon joining. They also receive a Membership Certificate, Club Bookmarks and regular Book Club Bulletins.

We hope you enjoy this book. Your friends will enjoy it, too. If they are not already members, why not ask them to join the WEEKLY READER CHILDREN'S BOOK CLUB.

WEEKLY READER
Children's Book Club
EDUCATION CENTER, COLUMBUS 16, OHIO

CONTENTS

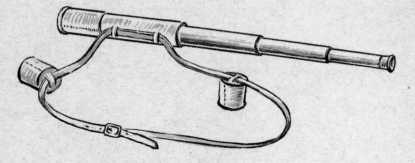

Chapter One

THE RAGGED OLD MAN

Davie stopped at Mr. Buchanan's shop and pressed his nose against the window to look in at the telescope. It was a beauty, right enough! Like new—better than new, for the leather case had been cleaned and polished and oiled and rubbed until it shone. Whoever owned it had taken real good care of it.

"It surely is the finest glass in the north of Scotland!" thought Davie. How could a body part with it and put it up for sale!

He put his school books on the stone ledge and cupped his hands beside his eyes so he could see better. There were no lights in the shop because old Mr. Buchanan never opened up much before noon except on Saturdays.

What a glass to have, all a person's life, for finding sheep on the hill, and keeping an eye out for a wildcat. Or for stalking stags. A good glass and a good dog, that's what a shepherd needed, here in the

Highlands. Oh, and stout boots and a good eye in your head too, of course. There was so much for a shepherd to know about his hill and his sheep and the weather and all. But a good dog and a good glass— aye, a fine glass like this one—that would be a fair enough start.

Davie glanced at Mr. Buchanan's big clock and gathered up his books and ran . . . and crashed hard into something big and solid and smelling of tweeds and tobacco. Davie went sprawling on the sidewalk and the big man staggered back and almost fell on top of him.

It was Sandy Big Alec!

"Hisst boy! Ya clumsy . . . ! Don't ye ever watch, now, where ye're going? . . . . ."

Sandy Big Alec! Of all people to be bumping into! Davie didn't dare to look at him and scrambled to pick up his school books and his lunch box, scattered all over the street. But he knew Sandy Big Alec's eyes would be on him, and his fat red face would be dark and scowling.

Davie mumbled that he was sorry and hurried off as fast as he could toward the school.

Sandy Big Alec—everyone called him that and never Mr. Mac-Murchie. He'd been looking in the window too, at the telescope. Och yes, and he'd be wanting it too, for you couldn't pass the shop without seeing what a bonnie glass it was. If Sandy Big Alec was wanting the glass he'd get it sure, being well off and accustomed to buy up what he fancied.

Once in a while in summer Davie and his father would meet Sandy Big Alec with his two champion sheep dogs, far up on the hill where their lands ran along side by side on the bleak top of Craig Dhu.

Father would lean on the stone dyke and call out, "Good day, Mr. MacMurchie!" But as often as not Sandy Big Alec would say, "Good, is it? There's rain squalls coming up as'll wet you through before you're home." Or he'd growl, "Och, now! It cannot be a good day when I've lost thirty lambs since March!" Sandy Big Alec was like that. Sour usually, and looking for the unworthy thing to say about a person. Sometimes at the Dog Trials Sandy Big Alec would laugh a bit over his mug of tea, especially if his dogs had run well, but most times he was a dour man.

He had lost the lambs all right. They had *all* lost lambs the last two or three years. Father and Sandy Big Alec and Piper Rory McLeod lost them on the hills and screes of Craig Dhu where their lands came together. But Sandy Big Alec could afford to lose them more than

3

Father could. If Father lost any more lambs, he'd not have the money for the rent of the croft, Mum said. He'd have the rent money no doubt, but it was a serious thing to lose the lambs.

It was a mystery where the lambs went. Oh, someone had stolen them all right for there was no trace of them. A wildcat would have left plenty of tell-tale traces and if dogs had worried them to death they'd be there lying dead on the hill somewhere. They hadn't fallen into the burn either.

When Davie reached the Post Office he turned to see where Sandy Big Alec was. Sure enough he was still there, looking in Buchanan's window at the glass.

Davie walked the whole length of the main street of Rothiemore on his way to school, past all the shops which were just opening their doors for the day's business. The two garages opened early to serve the tourists on their way up to Inverness on the Great North Road. The hotels were stirring too, the "Duke of Gordon" and "The Green Firs." The "Duke of Gordon" always had some big expensive cars drawn up in front of it, bigger cars than the ones at "The Green Firs."

People said the country was beautiful around Rothiemore, but the tourists hurried through it, not having much time to spend it seemed. Unless they had to stop for petrol or stay overnight, Rothiemore didn't delay them very much and they were soon out of the village on the winding road beside the River Spey.

Davie thought it was beautiful. He would rather live there than anywhere else in Scotland, anywhere else in the world for that matter. He hadn't really been anywhere else, except up to Inverness twice, and last year when he drove down to the sheep sales at Perth with Father and Dan Dory.

Around the corner past McKinnon's and The Woolen Store was the school. Iain McLeod and young Andy Grant were standing at the corner, laughing and giggling, and a dozen other school children were buzzing and swarming in the lane at the side of The Woolen Store.

And shuffling along the side of the road was old Billy Bayne, the tramp. He was singing. But though his voice was surprisingly loud and carried easily to the ears of housewives busy in their kitchens, nobody seemed to be coming out with a penny or a bit of breakfast for the old man.

> "The bonnie Prince is come awa-a-ay
> Away on the wave from the heather so green
> Nor house, nor home in this country has he
> And Flora has tears in her een."

"What's he been doing?" said Davie to Murdock MacIvor.

"Oh nothing. Just singing his songs. He slept in Gentles' barn all night. Margaret told me when I came by."

"Did they give him his breakfast?" asked Davie, feeling sort of sorry for the poor old man.

"No, they didn't. They didn't have time. They were going to Inverness this morning."

"He's raggeder than ever!" said Davie.

> "Many a heart will break in two
> Should he ne'er come back again.
> Will ye no' come back again, young sir,
> Will ye no' come back again?
> Better loved you'll never be
> And will ye no' come back again?"

Old Billy had on the same old Tam O'Shanter with the tartan band and ribbons streaming down behind. And the same old tattered macintosh held together in front by one button and a safety pin. The pockets of the ragged coat bulged with packages and bundles all mysterious—odds and ends wrapped in fragments of brown paper. His toes were sticking out between the broken leather of his boots and he had bags tied around his ankles like lumpy leggings. What was in his pack nobody knew.

Old Billy stopped singing and looked around to see whether any of the children might have a penny or two. His little dark eyes were bright and shining above his rosy cheeks, and his great grey-white beard bristled out all round his face and mingled with the matted hair that curled out from under his cap like sheep's wool.

If any of the children had pennies, they weren't going to give them up to old Billy Bayne. They just stood there, giggling and snickering, but not too loud because old Billy sometimes got cross and whacked at you with his stick if he thought you were teasing him.

Then Davie saw that he had a dog with him! A wee dog on a rope. He had never had a dog with him other times when he came begging through Rothiemore. It was a nice wee dog too, but fearful thin. It looked about six months old perhaps, and mostly black with a white muzzle and shirt front, and a white tip on his tail.

"Are they teachin' you proper at school now?" old Billy called out, to no one in particular. "Are they tellin' ye true about Bonnie Prince Charlie and the '45? They musn't be forgot. Have ye got a penny for a poor old man, any one of ye?"

"Where'd he get the wee dog?" whispered Davie.

"Och, stole it for sure. Else where would old Billy get a dog?"

"It's a bonnie wee dog," said Davie, "but dreadful thin."

Mrs. Morrison opened the door at the side of The Woolen Store and shook her mop into the street. She looked at old Billy and old Billy looked at her, but she didn't smile or offer him a bite so he began another song—

> "On the heights at Killiecrankie
> Yester-morn our army lay . . . . "

Murdock MacIvor and Iain McLeod and the other boys ran off

toward the school, and yelled a jeering "Ya-a-a!" when they were at a safe distance from Billy's stick.

Davie turned and ran too. But when he had gone a few steps he stopped and looked back at the old tramp and his puppy. Old Billy had stopped singing right in the middle of the third verse of "The Braes o' Killiecrankie." The children had run away, Mrs. Morrison had shut her door and no one else came out to hand him some pennies or bread and jam. He stood there in the roadway scanning every window and door for a friendly face, but there was none. The wee dog just sat there at Billy's feet looking hungry and sad.

Davie watched the old man shuffle along the street and turn up the lane beside the schoolyard. My, but he was ragged! Surely never in years had anyone cut his hair! But those little sharp eyes of his didn't miss much, mind you.

When old Billy had limped slowly up to the top of the lane and turned out of sight, Davie followed to see where he would go. Perhaps he would open his bag. No one had ever seen what was in the bag old Billy carried.

The old man had disappeared when Davie got to the top of the lane. Out beyond, there was just an open field as far as the railway track. Davie ran a few steps to see where he could have gone, and then he was startled to find himself standing right beside old Billy, close enough to get a swat with the stick if Billy had a mind to!

He was sitting down in the sun, with his back propped against the schoolyard wall. Davie blushed red, being caught like that, unexpected —old Billy and the dog both looking at him. He didn't know what to say, but he had to say something.

"Good morning, Mr. Bayne!" Davie said at last.

"*Mister* Bayne! Well now, that's a polite lad. On your way to school, I guess, eh?"

"Yes sir, I must . . . . "

"Aye, it is a good fresh morning. Aye, but not a good day for us, the wee dog an' me. No one wants to give us a bit this day from their plenty, not even so much as a bowl of porridge or brose, let alone sixpence. Do ye have a penny maybe?"

"No, not here I haven't," said Davie.

Old Billy looked very tired. He reached into the pocket of his tattered macintosh and found what looked to be a dirty crust of bread. The puppy looked at it longingly but old Billy stuffed it into the hole in his great white beard where his mouth should be.

"Boy," he said, "it's fearful hard for an old singer these days in

Scotland, and seldom a generous gift or a meal. Men's hearts have cooled and hardened since the days o' the bonnie Prince. There isna warmth or magic any more. I'm sick, boy! I've been to the Healing Well at Culloden but no good has it brought me. I'm sick and ailing, lad."

Yes, he looked tired and sick, for all the brightness in his eyes.

9

"Och, I'm afraid I'll have to turn in somewhere. And I haven't had to do that in thirty years o' walkin' from the border to John O'Groats."

"But in the winter . . . . ?" began Davie.

"Oh no. In the bitter cold months o' winter I go to Perth where there's a home that takes me in and gives me a warm bed. I can go there now indeed . . . . Sleepin' in a bed in Perth! When the bonnie winds o' summer are on the highlands . . . . . Och, I'd as soon die altogether!"

"What's the wee dog's name?" Davie patted the collie's head and rubbed his lean ribs.

"Fly, I call him. Fly's a good name for a fast young dog and it carries on the wind so's the dog can hear ye." Old Billy pulled Fly's head around. He was rough with the dog, but old Billy had never had a dog before, most likely.

"He'll be a fine dog this one. A remarkable dog! A level headed dog! See the keen eye he's got." Old Billy leaned over toward Davie as though whispering a secret. "Hist lad! Do you know . . . this one's descended from Old Hemp, and ye know yourself, there's never been as fine a dog in Scotland as Old Hemp!"

"Old Hemp!" exclaimed Davie, and whistled. "Old Hemp! Well!" He looked at the wee dog again to see whether he looked anything at all like a champion Trials dog. But Fly didn't look much different than a hundred dogs around Rothiemore. You can never really tell though, by a dog's looks, whether he's a useful dog on the hill or a winner at the Sheep Dog Trials. Handsome is as handsome does, with sheep dogs.

Old Billy eased himself into a more comfortable position against the wall. The sun was full out now and it was warm there out of the wind. Davie put his school books on the ground and opened the strap on his lunch box.

"A . . . a . . . if you'd be wanting a sandwich . . . ." he stammered, holding one out to the tramp. Old Billy opened his eyes quickly enough then, and lost no time in making a good half of the sandwich disappear in one mouthful.

"Numble-blum-m . . . thank ye, lad!" The old man's words were muffled by the whiskers and gobbling up the sandwich. It disappeared so quickly that Davie took another from his box and gave it to old Billy before he closed the lid and buckled the strap. But then he caught sight of the hungry look in the eyes of the wee dog Fly, and he could do nothing else but open the strap again and give the last of his sandwiches to the dog. He felt that Billy should have given the puppy a bite of *his* sandwiches because after all Fly was *his* dog. But he hadn't.

Davie shut the lunch box and pulled the buckle tight. Now there were only two oatmeal cakes left inside it, and that was all the lunch he would have at noon. Well . . . well, he was glad that old Billy had the sandwiches, and he was glad he had given one to the wee dog even though it *had* disappeared in two gulps into the narrow hungry space between the puppy's ribs.

"And your name lad? Are ye a shepherd's lad, or a gamekeeper's? Ye're not a village lad?" The food seemed to have revived the old man.

"Matheson, sir. My name's Davie Matheson. And we've a croft farther up the valley, two miles or more away, beyond Truim Barracks. Crubenbeg Farm, it's called."

"Och, I knew ye weren't a village lad. Here in Rothiemore a body meets with grudging kindness, and the lads are saucy. Beyond Truim Barracks ye live? You know Truim Barracks then and all the story of it?"

"Aye, I've been to Truim and heard the stories."

Old Billy sat up and pointed with his stick. "See now! You can see Truim from here. There were sheep stealers caught there thirty years ago, using the ruins to hide away."

"There's sheep stealers about now," said Davie, "and not caught either."

"There are? Ye'd do well to look in Truim then. There's old vaults and cellars there, and secret caves thereabouts, I've heard said."

"I don't think they'd be there, the sheep stealers. There's tourists go there sometimes, and people hiking about the country."

Old Billy leaned back against the wall and stretched out his legs. The soles of his boots were worn right through. He had stuffed paper in the holes but that was worn through too.

"A sad place, those ruins. There was a grand castle there in Scotland's great days. A stronghold. Truim Castle it was then. But it was laid in ruins by the English and the barracks built to awe the clans. There's been many things happen at Truim—some o' the poor broken lads gathered there after the battle of Culloden, till young Prince Charlie sent a message that the cause was lost, and they should go home.

"Aye, years ago I slept sometimes at Truim. But no more! For one night a fearsome thing happened. It wasna a dark night either, nor misty, but the whole land flooded with bright moonlight. I had just snuggled up warm in a corner to sleep . . . .

"Suddenly from the north, there came the sound of the pibroch and marching men. I flung my plaid about me and ran to a break in the ruined wall. There wasna a man in sight—nothing, save the moonlight bright as day and the trees standing black on the moor. But the din kept up, and became the sound of battle—the clash of metal on metal, of sword against shield, and the hoarse yellings of the men, an' the wild skirl o' the pipes urging them to the fight. It was plain to hear the struggle was hot and wicked!

"Och, I was filled wi' fear and horror so that I could not move! Then the weird battle died away an' stopped, and I heard the sound o' marching men coming over the moor across the heather. Louder and louder it grew, but still I couldna see a moving thing! Then the ghost army—or whatever it was—passed *clean through* Truim, so close to me that I might ha' touched them, had they been there at all. First the pipers skirling, and then a long straggle o' talking, yelling men. The sounds grew fainter and finally died away an' the night was still as before. An' d'ye know the day it was? The 16th of April, the dark day of Culloden! From that night I never slept again at Truim."

Davie nodded. "It must have been fearful! I've heard other tales of the place too, from my mother, and there's some folks won't go near Truim at all, let alone at night!"

All this time Davie had been kneeling on the grass and the wee dog was nuzzling Davie's hands with his wet nose, and wriggling all over with friendliness. He was hoping for more food no doubt, but he seemed hungry for friendliness almost as much as for food.

"The poor wee beast has taken a fancy t' ye," old Billy said, hauling him away by the rope.

"Aye," said Davie.

School! Davie had forgotten school, forgotten the time, forgotten everything, he had been so taken up with the ragged old man and the dog. He was late. There were no sounds coming from over the wall; the children had gone into school. He'd be very late!

He didn't say another word to Billy Bayne or the dog. As he ran back down the lane his feet felt like lumps of lead, and his heart was sinking like lead too. He'd catch it for sure! The other boys would be certain to say that he had been right outside, or at least Murdock Mac-Ivor would. He'd have to go to Mr. Rennie's office. There would be explanations to make and extra work to do. Perhaps he could do some of it at noon hour to make himself forget about feeling hungry.

It was even worse than that! When Davie reached the school door Mr. Rennie was standing there talking to Miss Grant, his teacher.

Mr. Rennie looked at Davie over his glasses. "David Matheson, it seems that you have been wilfully late," he said sternly. "I'll talk to you in my office."

Chapter Two

PRINCE CHARLIE'S CAVE

Davie opened his eyes and yawned. It was Saturday at last and he could lie in bed awhile longer if he wanted. He was glad enough there was no school today. All his spare time on Thursday and Friday had been taken up with the extra work Mr. Rennie had given him to do because he'd been late. *"Wilfully* late," Mr. Rennie said. Old Billy Bayne and the dog were nowhere to be seen in Rothiemore since Thursday.

The turkeys set up a noisy gobbling and chirping beside the kitchen door, which meant that Mum was out feeding them their morning mash, and it must be nearly nine o'clock. He couldn't lie there too long, because there were always more things to be done on Saturday than a body had time for. In the morning there were always chores around the house. And old Mrs. Finlayson in the shepherd's cottage down the road had a message for him to do some time. Everyone called them "messages," but they were really errands—going to the village for some groceries, or taking a parcel to post, or sometimes delivering a few orders of meat for Mr. Fleming the butcher when there were too many for his regular boy, Jamie Dermott.

After dinner he was going to meet Iain and go up to the old bothy or maybe to the shinty game at Gowie's field. Almost always at this time of year there was a shinty game on Saturday afternoons at Rothiemore.

Davie kicked off his covers and slid out of bed. His bedroom was far from tidy. Mum was always scolding him for dropping his clothes anywhere when he went to bed. By the end of the day, you were so tired that hanging up coats and laying out pants and stockings was just too much to expect.

It was a windy day, but clear—even some sunshine breaking through the ragged clouds here and there. The Cairngorm Mountains were blue-black along the horizon to the north with all the broad valley of Strath Spey in between. Birch trees and pines crowded down from the glens into Strath Spey like marching armies sweeping across the moors and the heather. It was a restless looking valley, aye, and restless it was in the days when the clans had gathered for Prince Charlie in the '45 and been defeated. The chieftain of the valley, Cluny Macpherson, had hid himself in those hills for nine years while the royal forces searched for him. But they did not find him.

Davie could see Truim Barracks from his window, and a few of the houses in Rothiemore. Perhaps they *should* look in Truim Barracks for the sheep stealers, he and Iain, this afternoon. People said Billy Bayne was nothing but a poor daftie, but he observed a lot with his bright little eyes and there was truth sometimes in what he chattered about.

15

"Davie! Morag!" Mum called upstairs when she came in from feeding the turkeys. "Are you coming now? I want to get the dishes away and off the table. Hurry down now; you've had a good sleep!"

Mum was ladling out the big spoonfuls of brose into their bowls when Davie came down. The stone floor was cold on his feet.

"Put on your stockings and boots, Davie," Mum scolded. "You

shouldn't come down to breakfast like a wild creature. Have you washed?"

"Yes, Mum."

Morag was at the table already, waiting to say the grace. Davie liked real thick porridge better than brose. There was no better way to start the day. "Puts a lining on your stomach," Father said. But Mum had been busy last night and hadn't time to put porridge in the black iron pot on the stove.

Aunt Flora—she was really Father's auntie—was in her rocking chair by the window starting her day's rocking, but little Christie wasn't down yet. She was only five and a real sleepy head in the mornings. "I declare, I don't know what I'll do when Christie starts to school and I'll have to get three of you off on time in the mornings!" Mum was always saying.

Father had his breakfast over and was out on the hill already with Moss and Sweep, the two sheep dogs. Father was worried about losing the lambs.

"It's a queer mystery, those lambs," said Mum. She whisked one of the cats from the chair and sat down to her third cup of tea. "They must have been taken from Craig Dhu or back somewhere between Craig Dhu and Loch Laagan, for we all lost some when they were taken, Mister MacMurchie and Piper Rory and us. But Craig Dhu is so far from a road. It's a lonely place however, where they could gather the sheep without anyone knowing."

"There's gypsies camped near Rothie Bridge," Morag said. "Two caravans of them."

But Mum shook her head. "There's been too many taken to be the work of tinkers or gypsies. It's been someone that took them off to market."

It was one of the worst of all sins to be thieving sheep here in the highlands. Years ago sheep stealers were hanged for their crime.

17

Davie finished his brose and spread blackberry jam thick on a slice of bread. "Old Billy said we should have a look about Truim Barracks, and maybe we will this afternoon, Iain and I," he said.

"Och, old Billy Bayne, poor daft old man!" said Aunt Flora, in her reedy voice. "I should think you'd have had enough of him Davie, to be sure. Why, I mind thirty years ago he was wandering about, blathering the same way and singing his old songs."

"Well, perhaps we *shall* search around the Barracks, nevertheless!"

Morag agreed with Aunt Flora. "They shouldn't let him just tramp around the country like that. They should put him somewhere and make him stay."

"It's a bonnie wee dog he's got with him this time," said Davie.

"Yes, and where'd he get it? Fair and honest do you think?"

"Aye, he said it was given him to settle a debt."

"Settle a debt! Who would owe Billy Bayne anything! He hasn't all his wits, and he's never done a tap of work."

"He sings for his supper."

"Aye. Aye. Croaks his old songs and sleeps in byres and fancies he's gathering help for Prince Charlie!"

"Mum . . . where does old Billy Bayne come from? Was he really a schoolmaster once, in Edinburgh, like some people say?"

Mum began to clear away the breakfast dishes. "I do wish you wouldn't argue so about everything, you two children. Nobody knows very much about old Billy. *Maybe* he was a schoolmaster once. *Maybe* he got the dog honestly. It's a collie, is it?"

She mixed up some bread and milk for the cats. There were always a lot of cats around the kitchen at Crubenbeg. When the big porridge pot was on the stove it held enough for all the family and for the dogs and cats as well. There were eight cats just now, crouched around the basin with their tails standing straight up in the air. The kitchen was big and there was plenty of room for them on the flagstone floor and

on the window sills among the plants and on any chairs not being used by people. In the summer Mum always left the window in the scullery open so that cats could come and go as they liked.

"Do you think old Billy's dog could really be descended from Old Hemp?" said Davie. "He's a sharp wee dog, and if he *were* from Old Hemp, he could be trained into a champion."

"Margaret Gentles said he *must* have stolen it," said Morag.

"Maybe he did and maybe he didn't," said Davie.

"It isn't likely he cared much whether it belonged to anyone proper," put in Aunt Flora, "and little training the poor creature will get from Billy Bayne!"

"Some day I'll have a dog of my own," said Davie, "and we'll practice for the trials."

"Ay, you'll have a dog, Davie," laughed Mum, giving him a pat on the cheek. "You can run him in the trials, and he'll help Moss and Sweep on the hill when they get old."

When he had finished sawing sticks, and had filled the big box by the kitchen stove Davie went down to the lower pasture with Morag and Christie to play in the tree house. They had placed a ladder against the great gnarled trunk of an old beech tree and gathered a lot of broken pots and kettles and pieces of board to set up housekeeping in the lower branches and on the big roots of it. Sometimes it was a laird's castle, or the highland stronghold of Cluny McPherson; sometimes it was just a plain house.

Davie liked it better when it was a highland stronghold, but the girls would have it nothing but a house today. After awhile Davie grew tired of it and wandered off down the meadow toward the stream. Down here the burn was quiet after its headlong dash through the rocky glen from General Wade's bridge.

All at once he noticed that something was bothering the ducks over at the other side of the pasture. It was a dog, rounding up the six bewildered ducks and chivvying them this way and that. It was Fly, old Billy's Fly!

The poor ducks were getting tired, but the puppy was having a wonderful time, driving them along and then racing around in front to bring them to a halt; edging them one way and then another, then holding them together in a tight little flock.

Davie smiled to himself. "Aye, he's a born sheep dog! A good one! Perhaps he *is* descended from Old Hemp!"

A short length of rope was trailing from the puppy's neck. Davie ran over and caught it, and saved the six ducks from further trouble.

"You haven't hurt them at all, that's good," Davie said to the wee dog. "Now where's old Billy? Have you left him or is he somewhere about?"

He looked all around but saw nothing of the old man. Davie was sure, though, that the tramp wasn't far away, for the dog would stay by him even though old Billy didn't treat him very well.

Then he thought, "He's in the cave! He's in Prince Charlie's cave!" and they ran downstream, Davie and the dog, until they came to the stepping stones where they could jump across the burn.

Prince Charlie's cave was a rather hard place to reach. It was in the side of the bank by the brown pool at the foot of the glen. You could not get to it when the water was high, but now in summer there was a narrow ledge at the bottom of the bank where you could creep along to the mouth of the cave. You couldn't see there was a cave at all, for the alder bushes grew up across the door of it. It was said that Prince Charlie hid there after Culloden when he was being hunted by the English.

Davie crept along the ledge and pushed aside the alder branches. Yes, there he was! Old Billy Bayne, sound asleep!

Billy Bayne's eyes opened at once when Davie stepped into the cave. He didn't speak for a minute, just blinked and frowned as though trying to remember where he was. Then he said—"Hello boy! Davie's your name, now. Davie Matheson. An' I willna forget it."

"I saw the wee dog in the pasture," said Davie, sitting on his heels on the rocky floor of the cave.

"Out looking for his dinner, like enough, while I was asleep. He didna take one of your chickens? No, he's learned no bad habits—exceptin' to beg his way in the world."

"He was just gathering up the ducks, sort of practicing. A good eye he has too, and eager."

Old Billy raised himself up on one elbow. The mouth hole in his whiskers stood open for a minute before he spoke. "I told ye he was from Old Hemp, didn't I. An' certain true it is, laddie! He's a real likely beast, like I said!"

"I thought you'd be here in Prince Charlie's cave when I saw the wee dog," said Davie.

"Prince Charlie's cave! Prince Charlie's cave, d'ye call it?"

"Aye, people say he took refuge here for a day or two, after Culloden, with Cumberland's soldiers hot on his heels. And a bonnie place to hide away, isn't it, being so hard to see?"

"It is that," said old Billy. "I never knew 'twas here till yesternight, with all the times I've been up and down the Great North Road! Prince Charlie's cave! Well, well!" The old man sat up and peered around in the dim light. "And to think I've been sleepin' here on the self-same spot the young Prince spent a troubled night or two!"

Old Billy lowered his voice to a whisper and looked about to make certain no one was near. He grasped Davie by the sleeve—

"Are you for Charles Edward? Are you for the fair Prince?" he whispered hoarsely.

"How can a person be for Prince Charlie when it all happened 200 years ago and more?" said Davie. Old Billy *was* a bit daft!

"Och, is it so long as that?" sighed the old man, running his fingers over his forehead as though brushing away the cobwebs. "Ah well, he was a bonnie lad, Charles Edward, an' he had the English full o' fear and on the run when he crossed the border. He'd have knocked the wee German lairdie off the throne if the clans had fought with him to the best of their strength. Aye, he would have."

Old Billy was breathing hard and his eyes had a glassy look.

"It hailed that April day, d'ye know boy, when the MacGillivrays and the MacLeans and Camerons and all died on Culloden Moor for Scotland and Charles Edward. All the brave clans routed in an hour, and the cause lost forever."

He seemed eager to go through the whole story as he had a hundred times before, no doubt, even though every highland schoolboy knows it all by heart—how the Scottish chieftains fought to drive King George the Second from the throne and restore the House of Stuart—how young Prince Charles Edward came from France, and the clansmen gathered round him to fight for the Stuart cause. But bonnie young

23

Prince Charlie never gained the throne and the hopes of all of them were crushed that day on Culloden Moor. That wasn't far away, Culloden Moor. The last time they had been to Inverness, Father took Davie and Morag to the wild moorland where the battle had been fought.

Old Billy started to sing, but softly this time, almost to himself—

"Tho' my fireside it be but sma'
And bare and comfortless witha'
I'll keep a seat and maybe two
To welcome Bonnie Charlie."

But then he stopped singing and he breathed a heavy sigh. "Ah, it's no use, laddie. Old Billy Bayne's defeated too, I fear. I've this sickness comin' over me . . . a real serious sickness, too, that couldn't be put right at the Healing Well in Inverness."

"Perhaps it's just that you're hungry, sir" Davie said, anxious to help the poor old man. "I'll run to the kitchen an' get a bite for you to eat. Or could you not walk up with me? My mother'll make you some gruel."

"No, no, laddie. I canna eat. I'm not hungry. Bye and bye y' might get something for Fly, poor thin dog. Then I must be gettin' out on the main road and beg a ride t' Perth, though I don't hold with ridin', when a man's got his own two legs to take him."

Billy Bayne picked up his boots. His toes and heels were gaping out of his socks even though he had on two pairs—or maybe three— of ragged woolen stockings. He got some heavy brown paper from the pocket of his coat and folded it carefully into the bottom of his boots to cover the holes.

"They'll take me in for awhile down in Perth, aye they will. But they won't take in the wee dog here. An' a good young dog he is, too. Did I tell ye now that he's descended from Old Hemp, and there isn't a better line o' dogs in all Scotland." The old man put his boots on and tied them together with cords all knotted and frayed. He wound the strings round and round his ankles.

"Now lad, hear what I have t' say—if I were to leave him with you, now, 'til I come back, ye'd look after him, wouldn't ye?"

Davie didn't know what to say. He looked down at Fly and the wee dog wagged his tail and flicked the red tongue in his laughing jaws. He seemed anxious to show that he agreed with old Billy—in fact, he'd be glad to stay awhile with Davie!

"Come now, laddie, ye'll have him now, won't you? And you'll train him too, eh? He's ready to be trained so ye'll have to do that. And ye mustna make a botch of it! Have ye a good dog yourself?"

"Aye, we've two good dogs, Moss and Sweep. Not the very best in trials maybe, but fine on the hill."

"Good, good! Then it's settled. Now d'ye think ye can find a few scraps for our dog? He hasna had more than a crust for the last two days."

"Aye. I won't be long." Davie scrambled along the edge of the bank and ran through the long grass beside the burn. The puppy was soon at his heels. "Come on then," Davie said, "we'll get something for old Billy too."

In the kitchen Mum and the girls listened to Davie's breathless story of old Billy being sick and spending the night in the cave. Fly tried to make friends with Christie and Morag and several of the cats all at once, while Davie hunted up some scraps for him.

"And he's entrusted the dog to you? Well now, I don't know about that, for it's awful hard to part with an animal once you've had him awhile at your heel. But we'll gather a parcel of food for the poor man and take him down a jar of hot tea. Why wouldn't he come up with you himself, to the house?"

When it was ready they all hurried down through the lower pasture,

Davie and the dog first, and then Morag with the stone jar of tea, and finally Mum with Christie by the hand. Mum had a shilling in her pocket, too. But when Davie reached the cave, old Billy was gone!

They searched all over for the old man, along the stream and up on the bank as far as the road, but he couldn't be found.

"I cannot understand how he disappeared so quick!" said Mum. "Someone must have picked him up at the road. But he'll be in Perth before long, for half the cars that pass south through Rothiemore are going to Perth and beyond."

"Look's like ye've got a dog for yourself Davie," said Father, when he came in from the hill and heard it all. "Aye, and a likely looking young fellow too, if he's fed a bit."

"I don't mind Davie having a dog for himself," Mum said, "but I don't care for it belonging to someone else, to come and take away when he chooses!"

Fly seemed happy enough with his fate. He settled down on the floor as though he belonged at Crubenbeg.

Davie felt all warm and happy inside. "He'll be a bonnie dog, if he's fed a bit—and trained," he said smiling.

Chapter Three

MIST ON THE MOUNTAIN

Every day the following week Davie hurried home after school and took Fly out for a ramble, along the rocky bank of the stream below General Wade's bridge or across the moor, and once halfway up to the top of Craig Dhu. He and dog were getting to know one another.

"You'll have to find out what sort of nature he has," Father told him. "Some dogs are touchy and sensitive, and there's some that need a lot of correction. And he's got to have confidence in you too, you know, before you'll do much with him."

Father knew a great deal about dogs. He had trained Moss and Sweep until they were as good hill dogs as any around Rothiemore. Father knew a great deal about everything. He was a quiet man most times, but there wasn't much he hadn't learned about all things living on the rocky hillslopes and moors in the highlands, whether it be sheep

27

or sheep dogs or rabbits or wildcats or men. He knew where to find the dotterel's nest, and there were very few people round about who had ever seen a dotterel's nest.

The next Saturday morning Davie awoke early and hustled down to breakfast. Morag and Christie were still sleeping. Even Aunt Flora hadn't come down yet. Father was finishing his egg.

Mum was at the stove, and having odd bits of breakfast between her kitchen chores. "Down already, Davie?" she said. "Yon Fly's getting you up earlier, I'll say that for him."

"I've to start training him in earnest. He's had nothing taught to him at all, tramping round with old Billy." Davie slid onto his chair and looked around at Fly. The puppy was wandering around between the cats near the door. He was looking better already with extra helpings of porridge and meat scraps every day for a week.

"Do you think . . . Father, do you think he's off to a bad start maybe . . . . you know, on account of Billy Bayne. He does nothing but chase rabbits, and won't come away at all, most times when I call him. And he's been worrying the hens."

Father smiled and shook his head. "Och, Davie, it takes patience, patience. Mischief in a puppy is a promising sign."

"I wish we'd seen Billy Bayne, and given him a pound or two for the wee dog so's he'd belong to Davie proper," Mum said. "If he trains the dog and keeps him for a year perhaps, it's not right that the old man should just walk in some day and claim him."

"Aye, maybe not, but that's the way it is," Father shrugged, and reached his cup across the table for more tea, "and anyway we've no pound or two to spare just now."

"Billy wouldn't have sold him for that!" Davie protested. "He's come down from Old Hemp, Billy says, and Billy's not so daft that he doesn't know Fly might be worth ten times that and more, when he's trained for the sheep."

28

"And the Trials," Father added, with a grin.

"Aye!" said Davie. "Aye . . . and the Trials!"

"The more reason why it's not right for old Billy to come back one day an' take him off with him." Mum almost wished Fly had gone to Perth with the old tramp a week ago, Davie could see, but she liked the wee dog.

"We're going down to the pasture this morning, Fly and me, and get down to work," Davie said. "He's got to learn to come in first of all. I'll try him on a check cord."

Father pushed back his chair. "Davie, how'd you and Fly like to go up to Piper Rory McLeod's? He's got four of our ewes who've wandered up the glen and must be brought back. Take Moss along with you. Your puppy'll maybe learn something from an old dog that's steady and sensible. I'll need Sweep myself."

Iain was not at home when Davie got to Piper Rory McLeod's. "Gone into Rothiemore with some messages to do," Mrs. McLeod said. "It's too bad. He might have gone back with you."

"Ye'll have a job on your hands," Piper Rory said, "to take home those wild young beasts. If you go straight over the shoulder o' Craig Dhu, it's only three miles which isn't far, but it's rough and steep. Perhaps it'd be best to go round by the road even though it be a good deal farther."

"Oh we'll go by Craig Dhu," said Davie, "we'll manage."

"And you'll be going through six hundred sheep of mine scattered out on the hill remember. It'll not be easy going through the midst o' them."

"We'll manage," Davie repeated.

"And why didn't ye bring Sweep along with you, instead of the fool puppy. What d'ye call him, Davie? I heard old Billy had left him with you."

"Fly's his name. He's from Old Hemp, Billy says." Davie wanted to

say something good about Fly because he'd been chasing Piper Rory's chickens too.

Piper Rory laughed. "From Old Hemp, d'you say? Well, maybe so. He looks likely enough, but dinna forget old Billy's wanting in wits."

Davie got the four sheep from their pen and started them out across the moor. Moss kept the ewes together, running first to one side and then the other, dashing ahead if they seemed to be trying to make a quick run for freedom, urging them on from behind if they slowed down or stopped to sulk. The dog was in full command of the sheep. He was enjoying it, running gloriously about his job, back and forth over the rough hilly ground and coming to Davie once in awhile to report that all was going well.

Fly wasn't very much help. He was enjoying it too—having a wonderful time, in fact—but often he did more harm than good. When Moss ran out to the left to head the sheep down a bank Fly raced at his side, but at the last moment he bounded right in on the sheep and sent them far in the wrong direction. Then Moss had to run a long half circle around to the other side to bring them back again.

"Well, he must learn," Davie thought to himself, and once in awhile it *did* seem as though Fly were taking a lesson from the older dog.

When Davie started out that morning with the dogs, the day was grey and overcast, and the clouds low so that the top of Craig Dhu was hidden in mist.

"I'm afraid it'll not clear up today," Father had said. "Davie, you may get a bit wet before you're back with the ewes."

There had been one or two sprinkles of rain on the way to Piper Rory McLeod's, but for the most part the air was still and heavy. For awhile Davie kept to a rough sheep track which led down the glen. A mile from Piper Rory's he swung over to the left, climbing up the steep shoulder of Craig Dhu. Around him the grouse kept up their persistent calling, which sounded like "go back, go back," but Davie followed steadily up the hillside after the sheep through the coarse grass and the gravel and the heather.

Here Fly became even more of a bother. Davie was shouting himself hoarse trying to bring him to heel. Even good old Moss lost his temper and took a nip at him once when he raced past and scattered the four sheep. Moss was trying to keep them headed up the hill for it was easier to hold them under control that way. Fly chased them up or down, it didn't matter which, as long as they were on the move. Davie would have given anything for a piece of rope to hold him; but even then, it might have been difficult to catch the puppy, for he was in the highest good spirits and paid no heed at all to Davie's shouts.

All along the slope of Craig Dhu, Piper Rory's six hundred sheep were sprinkled on the hill in two's and three's and half dozens, and it would have been the work of two good dogs to keep the four sheep from trying to join these others whenever there was an opportunity.

Here particularly Fly was a nuisance and Davie sometimes found he
was driving seven or eight sheep, counting those belonging to Piper
Rory which Fly had picked up and added to the little flock. Then he
and Moss would have to stop and separate the four ewes from the
others before continuing on the way.

As they made their way over the rough ground the mists began to
swirl around them. Davie tried to keep close behind the sheep and the
dogs. He couldn't run or the ewes would be driven too fast and make a
frightened dash. When they did they were hard to recover. "Never
mind, we'll soon be over the ridge and on our way down again, out of
the cloud," Davie thought to himself.

But the grey mist grew thicker, and the four sheep were becoming
jumpy and nervous. Fly was beside himself with joy at finding he could
make the ewes run any time he wished, or turn them to the left or to
the right. He didn't seem a bit tired of the game either. Davie's shouts

echoed around in the misty corries. He threw stones at Fly but couldn't hit the puppy or scare him off.

Moss was worried, for it was getting harder and harder to see the sheep and keep them together. Davie could see nothing now except the bracken and heather and boulders a few yards around them. Sometimes the mist would thin out and the top of a hillock appear but not enough to tell him exactly where he was. Nevertheless he was more concerned with keeping the four ewes than he was about getting lost.

He had lost all track of time. Up here in the grey mists on Craig Dhu, it was an eerie, ghostly world where there was no such thing as time or hours, or day or night, or any other animals or folk except Davie himself, the four ewes and the dogs. It must be far past noon however.

It was quiet too, silent, except for the muffled scuffling of the sheep as they scrambled along the sloping side of the hill.

Fly had been behaving himself for a few minutes, running along beside Moss with his tongue hanging out. But he was just gathering his resources for more mischief, for when one of the ewes strayed away from the others, Fly made a wild dash after her. He sent the frightened ewe scampering off down the hill and in a moment sheep and dog were lost from sight.

Moss made an effort to head them off, but he knew that if he went too far away the other three sheep would be lost too. He looked hopelessly at Davie and had to work desperately to keep the rest from charging off after the runaway.

The mist was very thick now. Davie shouted after Fly and stumbled a few steps following them, but the puppy paid no heed to him of course. He couldn't see Moss either, but he could hear the sheep on ahead somewhere, frightened and running, and he knew Moss would stay with them as long as he could hold them together.

Davie stood still in the phantom world of drifting fog. He whistled from time to time hoping that Moss might hear his whistle and be able to bring the ewes round. Now there was no sound. Nothing moved. No hill or dyke or boulder could be seen. Davie was lost too.

He sat down on a mossy tussock to consider what was best to do. It had been a foolish thing to bring Fly along for "no pup should ever be run on sheep till you can stop him if you wish"—that's what Mr. Finlayson always said. Davie could have managed it with Moss well enough, if it weren't for the mist. Och well, it was too late to think about all that now.

Davie's coat was soaking wet from the mist, but it was heavy tweed and he was dry inside. It wasn't likely that the mist would lift so there was nothing he could do but try and find his own way home. He and Father would have to come back in better weather and find the ewes. Moss would be all right; he would turn up at Crubenbeg sooner or later. As for Fly, and where he would be found, no one could tell.

Davie set out down the brae—or what he hoped was down the brae. He *thought* he knew where he was, but there was no real way of telling, and there were so many valleys and hummocks on the side of Craig Dhu he couldn't be sure at all that he was going in the direction of Glen Truim. The ewes had led them on a very zigzag course through the mist.

He must have walked, or rather stumbled and slid, for half an hour without coming upon a single rock or dyke that he knew. Perhaps he had wandered around to Sandy Big Alec's side of Craig Dhu, and was descending into the valley of the Spey.

Then Davie became aware of something moving, ahead of him, coming toward him. A pebble was dislodged and rolled down the hill a few feet. He heard a snuffle and a snort, and there ahead of him in the mist stood five deer—five stags, standing still now, with their heads up, their ears out, and deciding what to do. Oh, they looked magnificent! Davie's heart was pounding. In another second they were gone, plunging away across the hill in the fog.

"Whew! Just wait till I tell Father!" Davie breathed.

It was surely a good place for sheep stealing, up here on the wild top of the hills, with plenty of corries where the sheep could be gathered together and high rocks from which a lookout might be kept. But how would they get the sheep to the road, so they could put them in a truck and take them out of the district to a market?

Presently Davie heard the sound of flowing water and came upon a burn rushing down a small rock cleft on the hillside. Here was something to guide him anyway. If he followed the burn he would soon come out somewhere in a valley, whether it was Strath Spey or Glen Truim.

He was beginning to feel very hungry too, and it made him hurry in his scramble down the slope. The small burn joined a larger stream. Davie was pretty certain now that this was the River Truim, and sure enough, he soon recognized the moors above the bridge, and saw the stone arch of General Wade's bridge looming up in the mist. He was nearly home!

So the mist had come right down over the valley! Mum would be worrying about him.

Sweep heard Davie coming up the lane and ran to meet him. It was good to see the flat grey shape of the house at last, and to think of it being dry and cheery inside and about the dinner that would soon be on the table for him by the warm stove.

When Davie pushed open the kitchen door the first thing he saw was Fly!

"Yes, Fly!" said Mum. "Och, I'm glad you're home, Davie lad! When Fly came back awhile ago, all by himself we began to fret about you!"

Father had been putting on his coat when Davie entered. "I was just going out to have a look for you, with Sweep," Father said, looking relieved. He hung his coat on its peg behind the door. "Is Moss not with you? Tell us what happened, now."

"It's nearly time for tea, not dinner. Half-past three. You must be starved, Davie!" Mum shoved some sticks into the stove and opened the damper. She put the pot of stew on the fire. "We'll warm up the hotch-potch, and I'll make some stovie tatties for you. Morag, set the table now, will you, like a good girl."

"Here Davie, give us your coat," Father said. "I'll hang it here by the fire. And sit down yourself close by it to get dry and warm. You lost the ewes, no doubt, in the mist. How is it Fly's home without you?"

Davie sat in the rocker by the stove and told them what had happened.

"Never mind! You did your best, Davie," said Father. "A man can but do his best. And the stags! I wish I'd been with you. What a sight!"

"Moss was still set on the three ewes when I lost them," Davie explained, "but I cannot say much for the help Fly gave us."

Fly didn't seem to realize what a sorry showing he had made on the way from Piper Rory's. After nuzzling Davie's hand, he lay down heavily in front of the fire and closed his eyes. He was tired.

"You don't think so much now of your wee dog."

"Oh, he's . . . he's not had much of a chance yet," Davie said, rather half-heartedly, for he had been wondering to himself, coming down the brae through the mist, whether a dog that hadn't shown any more natural sense than Fly would ever amount to anything at all.

Aunt Flora stopped her knitting and said, "Like as not he's one of those dogs that unduly chases the sheep, or lacks a cool head. Och, an' I've seen many a one you couldna do a thing with, no matter if you were to bawl your head off. Put in a lot of running about, they do, but get nowhere with it all." Aunt Flora always took the gloomy side of a matter.

"Fly's not had a chance yet!" declared Davie. "He's just a wee dog and over-eager to chase the sheep. You wait a while and see!"

"Aye Davie, if you lose heart the first try, you'll not be likely to get very far at anything," Mum said. "Come now, we'll have our tea, and Davie his dinner."

The stew and a cup of tea made Davie feel much better about the day. He had missed the shinty game at Rothiemore but then perhaps they hadn't played if the clouds had come down all over the valley. And Fly had at least had the sense to find his way home in the mist.

"It wouldn't be hard to gather up the sheep on top of Craig Dhu and steal them away, I was thinking," Davie said, when he had satisfied the worst of his hunger. "It's wild and lonely up there, and all hidden away."

"No, it wouldn't be difficult," Father agreed. "Maybe they're scared off now somehow and will take no more. The police are keeping an eye out for strangers on the roads."

"Ach, the police!" snorted Morag. "The police in Rothiemore are only Callum Campbell, who couldn't catch a rabbit—and sometimes Geordie Frazer to help him. Geordie Frazer's but a clumsy lout of a boy who works at the railway station too."

"Now Morag! Now Morag! Hold your tongue. It isn't easy for Callum Campbell. The sheepstealers'll get caught sooner or later, and little good their work'll do them."

Aunt Flora raised a bony finger. "I've heard o' thieving shepherds who have trained their collies to do the mischief all by themselves. They would point out the sheep to their dogs and then go and visit their neighbours while the sheep were being stolen, so as not to be suspected of it."

"Aye, but the dog wouldn't be to blame," said Davie.

"Oh no," Mum said, "the poor dog wouldn't ken the right and wrong of it."

"I'l train Fly on the check cord for a bit," Davie said, "until he minds what I say."

"Perhaps so," said Father. "It's a long journey you have. Don't be harsh with the wee dog, and don't forget to praise him when he does what's right."

They had finished their tea and the dishes were cleared from the table, when there was a scratching at the door. Then a whine. Father and Davie looked at each other and Davie hurried to open the door.

"It's Moss!" he cried. Moss whined again, but didn't come in to the kitchen. Instead he ran away a few steps and waited. In the mist beyond him, guarded by Sweep, Davie could see the ewes.

"He's brought in the ewes!" Davie shouted. "*All four* of the ewes!"

"Bless me, so he did. All four!" said Father. "Now there's a proud dog for you!"

Chapter Four

TRAINING THE SHEEP DOG

Davie knew that it was going to be a long and difficult job to train Fly. Some young dogs seem to pick up their lessons without any trouble at all, while others are always doing the wrong thing—or worse still, doing nothing at all. Really it was very much like the girls and boys at school who either found it easy to remember their arithmetic and geography or had a hard time learning things however dutifully they plodded along and did their best.

It was clear from the first that Fly didn't always do his best. He was too fond of play and excitement to settle down to doing his work quietly and well. A sheep dog has to have all his wits about him if he's going to handle the sheep properly and make them respect his commands.

He has to know just how far he can edge forward toward the sheep so that they will turn and move in another direction, and not be frightened into mad flight. On the way from Piper Rory's, Fly had sent the four ewes flying a score of times and each time it took a long while to gather them up again and calm their nerves.

A sheep dog has to know when to drop down on the ground and settle there for a moment or so, until the sheep collect their wits and decide what he wants them to do. And if they start charging off in the wrong direction he must move like a flash, in a wide circle, to get beyond them and steer them round. Oh yes, a sheep dog has to use his head and be very, very careful in his work.

"Yon Fly's got a natural knack of how to do things," Father would say, when he was watching the pup around the pasture, "if only he'd get over his feckless ways, and listen to a word or two of orders."

"Aye," said Davie. "First thing he's got to learn is to obey."

"It cannot be taught by being harsh with the wee dog, Davie. You won't put an old head on his young neck overnight."

So Davie settled down to it, and almost every day after school he took Fly out on the moor or to the lower pasture for some training. He took some tasty bits from the kitchen in his pockets too, so that the puppy would have a little reward when he obeyed orders.

First he took a stick with a clip on the end of it and fastened it to the dog's collar, so that he could keep Fly beside him as he walked. Fly was surprised at first, and not a bit happy to be held in check especially when they walked near the rabbit warrens on the hillside. Davie talked to him as they went along and very soon the puppy began to understand his words.

Sometimes instead of words he would whistle at the dog, one kind of whistle to stop and lie flat against the ground and another to get up and start on again. Then came the check cord, a piece of cord tied to Fly's collar instead of the stick. This gave the dog a lot more freedom but Davie could still keep him from dashing after the rabbits and could make him come in to him when he called.

Little by little Davie lengthened the cord and taught the dog new commands. He would give a long, hollow whistle, different from any of the others, which meant "Go out farther away from me!" If Fly paid attention to his lessons Davie never forgot the tasty bits he had in his pocket to reward the collie.

Oh but it was slow work, and it was hard for a boy to have the patience for it. Sometimes he felt like forgetting all about it and going off on a ramble up Craig Dhu to look for a dotterel's nest. Sometimes he got so cross when Fly seemed stupid or stubborn that he was tempted to hit him with the cord. But one thing certainly came of it—Davie and Fly got to know each other very well, and when half-past four came on school days Fly was always waiting there for Davie with a warm welcome which showed all over his black and white face, his wiggling body and his wagging tail.

"Coming on, coming on he is, Davie!" said Father. "I'm not sure he isn't a bit too much on the flibbetty-gibbetty side to make a good one for Sheep Dog Trials and such, but he'll be a fair enough help on the hill, if you persevere."

Davie shook his head. "If he'd only get over having his own ideas, I could make a Trials dog of him too, I think."

Davie did not like to admit it just then, but once or twice when he had slipped off the check cord and set Fly free to test him, the dog had been as bold and disobedient as could be. He had sent a flock of hens flying in a wild scatter down in the lower pasture, and yesterday on the hill he had chased off after a grouse and then slipped away home to avoid a scolding for it. He had left Davie standing on the hill whistling and shouting until he was hoarse and cross.

"I'll put some ewes down in the lower pasture for you, Davie," Father said, "and you can start him on the sheep."

42

Next day Father drove five black faced sheep down from the hill and put them in the pasture with Maudie and Tim the two farm horses. Fly was ready and eager to handle the sheep. He crept up to them boldly and even when one of the old ewes stood her ground and stamped her foot angrily at him, Fly didn't give way an inch. He would have given her a chase too, if it had not been for the check cord held firmly in Davie's hand.

And so it went on. Through May and into June Davie worked with the dog every day for an hour or two. They gathered the sheep and drove them this way and that across the pasture, and then tried to drive them into the small pen near the pasture gate.

It was a Saturday morning the first time they succeeded in getting the sheep into the pen. Davie swung the gate shut hard behind them and almost danced a fling, he was so happy about it. It happened too that Father and Andrew Douglas, the gamekeeper, were leaning over the fence talking, and Morag and Christie were peaking through the bars of it.

"Good, good!" cried Father. "Good lad! Your labour's not being wasted, Davie. You'll make a level-headed dog of that puppy yet."

"Aye, Davie! You're doin' good!" agreed Andrew. "Now try it without the check cord. He'll do it for you again, you'll see!"

Well, Davie was so happy about penning the sheep he thought he *would* try it. He opened the pen gate and drove the sheep down the pasture. Then he and Fly came back and stood by the fence near the two men.

"Now. We'll see how he'll do it!" said Davie. He stooped and loosed the check cord from Fly's collar and said "Whssht, Fly!"

Fly was away like a shot. He couldn't believe at first that he was really free from the check cord—free to put the sheep through their paces all by himself. But it was true!

"That'll do, Fly!" Davie shouted when the dog was nearing the sheep.

43

"Down Fly! Sit!" But Fly dashed on as though he had never had a day's training and drove the sheep fast across the meadow.

"That'll do! That'll do, Fly," cried Davie, and he whistled and shouted to bring the puppy to his senses. Fly heard every shout and whistle too. But he circled them hither and yon until the poor beasts were frightened and panting. For Fly, it was pure joy to make them run where he commanded.

Then he seemed to repent, and Davie, with much threatening and whistling, managed to make Fly bring the breathless sheep slowly up the pasture toward the pen. When he had them before the open door of the pen, he looked at Davie and waited for his orders.

But, as bad luck would have it, one of the ewes decided at that moment to make a break for the open pasture. It was too much for Fly. He raced after her and committed the sheep dog's greatest sin—he gripped the wool on the side of the ewe's neck in his teeth!

Davie shrugged his shoulders and sighed and walked away. He was heartsick at the foolishness of the wee dog. After all these weeks of training and trying——!

"Never mind, Davie," said Father. "It'll take a bit more work for us to bring him around to sense. I'll give you some help myself next week, me and Moss. Moss 'll show him how it's done. Never mind now, lad!"

Andrew pushed back his cap and scratched his head. "Not a thing wrong with the dog," he said, "save that he's over swell-headed. Just too high and mighty to stop when you tell him to stop."

Davie had no spirit left to say a word. He felt the tears in his eyes and blinked to hide them from the men.

"Ach, it's not a hopeless thing! No need to take on about it, Davie," Father went on. "I've seen much worse beginnings turn into grand hill dogs, haven't you, Andrew? But why don't you get your dinner now and go in to the shinty game this afternoon. Aye, and Mum's got a message for you to bring out to Mrs. Finlayson from Rothiemore."

Davie climbed over the fence and dragged himself slowly up the lane. He didn't even look around to see where the wee dog was.

It was a glorious shinty game they had that afternoon up at Gowie's field near Rothiemore, until the rain came down at half-past three. It came on suddenly—heavy, driving rain which sent everyone scurrying for shelter.

Davie ran to Mrs. Duthie's shop on the edge of the village. Mrs. Finlayson had asked him if he'd mind bringing some groceries for her on the way home from the shinty game.

The rain let up a bit, but still he was soaking wet when he reached the Finlayson cottage.

"Come in, come in, Davie!" said Mrs. Finlayson. Her welcome was always as warm as her fireside. "I declare, I never saw such weather in my life, as we have had this year. Wind and rain, and even hail awhile back. It's not a bit like summer at all. You can't go outside for a minute but you're soaked to the skin."

Mr. Finlayson was sitting in his comfortable big chair, carving on a hazel stick, and Annie was helping her mother with the tea things. Annie was almost a grown woman herself now.

"Mother's just afraid the bad weather'll persist into August, when she'll be at her cranberry and blueberry jam."

Mrs. Finlayson nodded. "We can't make jam if the fruit is wet. It's good and kind of you to fetch me these things, Davie. You'll sit down here with us for tea, for it's just ready this minute. I'll dry your coat by the fire."

"Been off playin' shinty eh, lad?" said Mr. Finlayson, looking up from his carving. "Och, I was great for shinty myself when I was a boy like you. Here now, what do ye think of this for a crook?"

He reached the stick scross for Davie to see. Davie took it and turned it over and over looking at the carving on the crook.

46

"It's . . . it's bonnie!" exclaimed Davie, and his eyes shone with admiration, for it really was about the finest shepherd's crook he had ever seen. A curving stripe swept round the whole length of the hazel shaft. On the top of the crook, perfectly carved, were a crouching sheep dog and two white ewes, all made of a ram's horn. The curve of the crook ended in a Scotch thistle. It was indeed a beauty!

"Aye, it's for the Rothiemore Trials, in August," said Mr. Finlayson. "Maybe ye'll be winning it with that young dog Fly of yours. I have to have it finished before we get too busy with the sheep shearing."

"He talks on, as if the carving on a crook made any difference at all in catching a tup by the hind leg with it!" said Annie.

Mrs. Finlayson bustled about with the teapot and cups. "Come now, we'll have our tea. We can draw the table up here so's Davie can stay by the fire and dry out. I have a bit of fish for our tea today. Do you like fish, Davie?"

It was always a friendly place, Finlayson's cottage. Davie felt almost like one of the family whenever he sat there in their cosy kitchen. Mr. Finlayson was shepherd for Lord Ennismuir, though it was Mr. Farquhar who managed the estate and they never saw much of Lord Ennismuir himself except in August when he came up for the grouse-shooting, and once in a long while during the stag season. Mr. Finlayson was always carving crooks or walking sticks in the evenings after a day's hard work. His was the finest carving for miles around, and he had won any number of prizes with his sharp knife.

"Tell us, Davie," he said, "how's the wee dog coming? Are you going to run him in the Rothiemore trials? You might do all right with him in the Novice Class."

"Oh no, I'll not run him in the Trials. He's not a trials dog, I'm thinking. Too headstrong. Won't listen to you when you tell him what to do. He's eager and all that, and Father says he'll make a grand dog for the hill, perhaps, if we persevere."

47

"Aye? Well then, that's enough, isn't it? Sheep dog trials are all right, but working with the sheep out on the hill that's the natural place for a collie. You want a dog that'll find your sheep when they're buried deep in a snowdrift, or 'll gather them up from all over the hill when you want to bring them down to the fold."

"There's some shepherds wouldn't be much good without their dogs to do their thinking for them," said Annie, teasing her father.

"That's right, girl! There's no shepherd could do very much without

48

a good dog or two. But I think I'd rather be a shepherd than a game-keeper for all that." Mr. Finlayson grinned and winked at Davie. Davie knew that Mr. Finlayson was joking with Annie because she and Andrew Douglas were fond of each other.

Annie flared up, pretending to scold. "Och yes, and where would you and your sheep be without a gamekeeper like Andrew to catch the foxes, and snare the rabbits, and keep down the weasels and wildcats and hoodie crows!"

"Well I'll grant you that, Annie! Gamekeepers are useful creatures. Now if they could only catch sheepstealers too, like they catch rabbits and foxes——. Davie, have you lost any more of your sheep over there on Craig Dhu?"

"No, I don't think so. Not the last while back. It's how the sheep-stealers manage to get them to the road where they'd have a truck and sheep float waiting, that's what Father can't figure out. They could gather them easy enough up there in the corries and hummocks. I'd like to catch them at it some day. If I'd a good dog and a glass. . . "

"Did you see the bonnie glass in Buchanan's shop in Rothiemore, Davie?" said Mr. Finlayson. "There's a glass for you now, all polished and kept!"

"Aye. I saw it there. Sandy Big Alec was looking at it."

"Och, he would be! And he'll get it no doubt, well-off as he is and neither chick nor child to save his money for."

"Most things he wants, he buys," Davie agreed. "It hasn't been in the window lately."

Mr. Finlayson thought for a moment. "Didn't Sandy Big Alec lose some of his sheep too, when yours were stolen?"

"Aye," said Davie, "he lost thirteen, he said."

"Mm. . . . well now, I don't see how the thieves could get them down this side from Craig Dhu over General Wade's bridge without you or Andrew Douglas knowing something about it. If they took the

sheep down the other side of the hill, they'd have to drive them between Sandy Big Alec's and Truim Barracks, an' it'd be queer then if
he didn't hear them."

"Sandy Big Alec was at the lamb sales in Perth," said Davie, "last
time we lost the sheep."

"In Perth he was? Ah well, 'think more than you say' is a good rule
to go by."

Mrs. Finlayson threw up her hands, "Och, now! Sandy Big Alec
wouldn't steal his own sheep! Nor do I think he'd steal anyone else's.
There's not many folks around Rothiemore will speak kindly of Sandy
Big Alec, but there's none thinks he'd steal a sheep. He's but a poor
selfish man."

"Selfish he may be, but not poor!" said Mr. Finlayson.

It was getting late when Davie crossed General Wade's bridge over
the Truim and climbed the rough lane to Crubenbeg.

His mind was full of things and running over. What a lot there was
to think about, what a lot of things happening, in the little bit of Scotland that was their own glen and the valley of Strath Spey around
Rothiemore!

Davie knew there was something wrong as soon as he pushed open
the kitchen door. Mum's face was clouded and anxious-looking. Morag
had been crying and her cheeks were streaked with dirt where she had
been rubbing her eyes.

Mum stopped what she was doing and turned to Davie. "Your dog's
been hurt, Davie," she said. "Sweep gave him a beating. Father has him
now, in the front room."

Davie had a dull, sinking feeling in the pit of his stomach as he
hurried through the hall to the living room. There was a fire going in
the fireplace, and in front of it Father was kneeling beside a box. There

was Fly in the box, lying on his side on an old quilt. He was a sorry sight! But he raised his head a little when Davie came into the room.

"He's all right now, Davie," Father said. "It was my fault. I took him on the hill with me, and Moss and Sweep too. He got rambunctious, and Sweep set on him to teach him a lesson."

Davie knelt beside the box and patted the wee dog's head.

"Ah, Davie, I wouldn't touch him now. He's sore and bruised all over. Your mother bathed his wounds and put some ointment on the bites. He'll be all right now though, if we keep him quiet in here for a bit."

Davie and the wee dog looked at each other, as though each wanted to say to the other, "Ah now, never mind. It'll be all right!" But Davie could feel the tears running down his cheeks.

"Sweep's not a sulky dog. I didn't think he'd do a thing like that," he said, sniffling and swallowing hard to keep from crying, really crying.

"Nor I. The young dog was rushing the sheep, and he sent them scattering when we were coming through the gate in the dyke. And Sweep just got angry at it, and thought he needed a lesson."

Father pulled the box a little farther from the fire. "His eye is cut, I think. He may lose the sight of it."

Davie sat there on the couch for a long time looking down at Fly, after Father went back to the kitchen. "It's a hard lesson he taught you," he thought to himself. "You're a bonnie dog, but too rash and hasty. Too rash and hasty for a Trials dog, though I was hoping y' might make a grand dog for the hill."

Then after a while Mum came in and said, "Come now, Davie. Come and have a bite of supper."

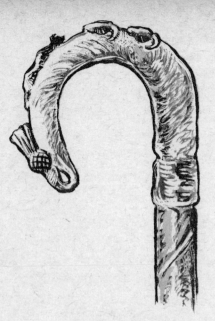

Chapter Five

THE ROTHIEMORE TRIALS

For a week Fly lay in the box on the old patchwork quilt. He didn't eat anything at all for three days, until one morning Mum tempted him out of his bed for some warm milk and porridge. He was so stiff and sore that he could hardly stand on wobbly legs. His eye looked red and terrible.

"He's blind in the eye now," Father said, "and I doubt if he'll see over much with it when it's healed up." Mr. Finlayson came over one evening with a bottle of milky liquid to bathe the eye, and it seemed to make Fly feel better.

"It's an old potion from the Hebrides," he said. "Meant for human beings, but if it is good for man it shouldn't hurt a poor beast."

On the next Saturday the dog ventured out into the kitchen, hobbling around the flagstone floor and nosing Aunt Flora and the two girls.

"Och I'll not give you any sympathy at all," Aunt Flora scolded. "A fool's got to pay for his folly. As a dog, you're as daft as your master. Now that's not meaning you, Davie, but Billy Bayne, for after all he's Billy Bayne's dog, is he not?"

"There's no one's heard a word of old Billy since he disappeared from the cave," said Mum. "Nor has he been seen anywhere along the Great North Road."

"That old man's tough as leather! He'll be back around one o' these days, mark my words, singing his trollolays and expecting bed and board for it."

Mum sighed. "Mm, aye! I'm thinking he will too."

Davie had been doing his best not to think about old Billy. Not that he had anything against the poor ragged tramp but he didn't like the thought of losing Fly. He had been a feckless puppy and a disappointment and all that, but Davie loved him just the same. And old Billy would never teach him anything, that was sure!

Whenever Davie looked back on it afterwards, he felt certain that Sweep and Moss noticed the change in Fly long before he did.

There was a week of warm clear weather, the first fine week of the summer, and Fly was getting over his wounds very quickly. Even his eye seemed to be healing, bathed each day with Mr. Finlayson's white liquid. It wasn't long before his stiffness disappeared and he was romping about almost as though nothing had happened.

Davie was afraid Sweep might still hold a grudge against the troublesome young dog, but they seemed to be friendlier than they had ever been before.

Strangest of all was the way in which Fly had suddenly become so much more obedient and sensible, instead of the rash, hasty puppy he had always been. When Davie called him, Fly came trotting. When Davie said "Steady!" or "That'll do!" Fly would stop and look at him. It was a sort of miracle!

"I cannot get over it!" exclaimed Father. "Why, the dog seems to have found his wits at last!"

It was true that Fly seemed to have decided to take things seriously, and not be a silly, feckless dog any more. So Davie began again to train the dog, out on the moor and in the lower pasture—teaching him to listen for commands and whistles, and to run out or drop down or creep forward when he was told.

Father put some sheep in the lower pasture, and in the evening he and Davie would take Fly and the two older dogs down to the meadow where they would spend an hour gathering the ewes and driving them and coaxing them into the pen.

"Moss is getting better all the time," Father said. "I think I'll run him in the Rothiemore Trials this year. He'd give Sandy Big Alec's collies a bit of competition, unless I'm mistaken."

There was another curious thing—before, it had always been Moss who had been patient and helpful when they had been trying to train Fly, but now it was Sweep who ran best with the puppy and showed him the tricks of the trade. And now sometimes Moss would get jealous of Fly and refuse to work with him; Moss would scorn the awkward young puppy and walk off to the other side of the pasture and sulk.

Father would laugh when this happened and call out, "Come on then, Fly! You show us how it is done! Good lad, Fly!" Oh, that would make Moss come in quick enough!

"I do believe it's Fly that's teaching Moss a thing or two. He's got to keep right up on his toes now or your young pup 'll have the job done before him."

There was a lot that Fly didn't know about handling sheep, especially when he found an old ewe which was stubborn or flighty. But he was learning and he was very eager now to please Davie. When he did something wrong he felt very badly, but there were times still when he would rush in too swiftly, for the sheer delight of seeing the sheep run.

"Patience, patience, Davie!" Father would say. "A dog must understand what he's doing. You don't want the blind obedience of a slave."

Davie was very pleased with Fly—a warm and comfortable feeling that seemed to fill his chest and rise up into his throat.

"He'll be a grand dog for the hill, won't he, Father—when he gets a bit older and settles down?"

Father stroked his chin, the way he always did when he was considering a serious matter. "Aye, he will. And maybe a Trials dog too, if you want. S'pose he keeps on, you might see how he'd do in the Novice Class at Rothiemore."

"In the Rothiemore Trials! This year?"

"Aye, next month!"

❋   ❋   ❋   ❋

The Rothiemore Sheep Dog Trials were held each year in August on the long hills beyond the village. They were just local trials of course, with shepherds and crofters from the district around Rothiemore and one or two dog handlers from the village itself, like Mr. Fleming, the butcher. Not like the big trials at Glenavon in September when the best dogs from everywhere in the north of Scotland were entered and even some from as far away as Ayrshire and Argyl. But there were some very good dogs right there around Rothiemore.

The posters were already up on the signboards and in the shop windows—

ROTHIEMORE
SHEEP DOG TRIALS
at Drumstaffen Farm
SATURDAY AUGUST 9th
commencing at 1 p.m.

Things looked so very different now that Fly had come to his senses and settled down to learn. But it was a long time before Davie could bring himself to think seriously of putting the young dog in the competition, even in the Novice Class. He probably would never have done it either, if Father hadn't just gone into the village and done it for him.

"I've entered Fly in the Trials for you, Davie. We don't want you to disgrace us all now, so the wee dog'd better know his lessons. I've entered myself too for the Shepherd's Cup, with Moss. We'll have to do our best, the both of us."

Usually Davie was counting the days until school would be over at the end of July, but this year he hardly thought about the end of term and the beginning of the holidays except that it gave him more time to practice with Fly in the clear bright afternoons of summer. He was counting the days until August the ninth, and he went up and looked at the hill on Drumstaffen Farm where the trials were always held.

August the ninth! What a day it turned out to be! Windy and full of fitful rain squalls, for one thing.

"Och, it's a shame!" said Mum. "Such day, when the weather has been so fair and bright for weeks!"

Morag had her face against the west window, where she'd been half the morning. "It looks brighter! Can't we go, Mum? It'll clear off, and anyway it's no different than going to school."

"We'll see, bye and bye. It'll be hard for the dogs to hear on a day like this, and Davie's whistle is not very loud. If Fly makes a foozle of it, Davie 'll be wishing there's nobody there at all."

It did stop raining, except for drifts of wet wind from time to time, but when they arrived at Drumstaffen Farm about half past one the wind was even stronger. The girls had come, of course, and Mum, but it was too far for Aunt Flora. "Anyway," Aunt Flora said, "I don't hold with dog trials much. The place for sheep dogs is on their own hill."

The trials had already started. Several dogs had run but none of them seemed to have done very well.

Davie had Fly on a leash beside him. He stopped on top of the little hill which overlooked the Trials and glanced around at the gathering.

Behind him was the winding, hilly road which came out from Rothie-more. A few people and bicycles were straggling along it on their way to the Trials. There were a dozen cars parked any old way at the foot of the hill.

On the front slope of the little hill were scattered seventy or eighty people—over a hundred perhaps if you included the small children and fifteen or twenty dogs.

It was still a dull grey day but the clouds were high now and only the lofty Ben Crichan had his head in the mist. The Twin Peaks were dark purple against the flat blue of more distant mountains and Davie could see the wind rippling across the silver waters of Loch Strome off to the right.

Just below was the tea tent, set up in a sheltered spot under the hill. And there were the three judges at their table—the tall man in the kilt was Captain MacPherson, but Davie didn't recognize the other two. When Davie looked at the judges so serious and the crowd all watching, he had a sinking feeling in the pit of his stomach. "Well. . . . come on, Fly!" he said, and went down to join Father near the judges' table.

"The next competitor will be Mr. Andrew Douglas with Lass! After that, Mr. Cowan with Nell!" the announcer called out through his megaphone.

Andrew took his dog out to the starting place. He was all dressed up in his best jacket and plus fours but he made sure not to look at Annie Finlayson standing by the tea tent. He was nervous already and that would have set him all a-tremble.

Andrew took his dog's head and pointed out the five sheep that were being driven over the ridge to the flag a quarter of a mile away. Lass finally saw them and Andrew sent her away with a loud "Whooshtt!"

Lass ran out very wide to get around behind the sheep—so wide that she seemed to have lost them altogether in the rough and hummocky hillside. But finally she found the ewes and circled round into position

59

behind them. There she sat down, and stayed down while Andrew bawled and bellowed and whistled into the wind. It seemed that Lass had felt her job was to guard the ewes, rather than to drive them down to her master.

After awhile Lass stood up and crept in toward the sheep, and they started down the side of the hill.

Everyone was occupied with watching the collie and the sheep and making comments now and then on the dog's performance.

"He's lost too much time now already!"

"They're comin' down too fast. Too quick, too quick!"

"Aye, they'll break!"

They *were* coming down too fast. In a wild flurry, they missed going through the first gate altogether. Andrew was shouting his loudest, his hands cupped beside his mouth to make his shouts carry against the wind, but Lass wasn't listening.

"Och, too much fuss! No good at all!" said a harsh voice, and Davie looked around to see Sandy Big Alec close behind him!

"Stop her! Stop her!" roared Sandy Big Alec, and then said, "Och, I knew it! I saw it comin'!" as the sheep broke and Lass chased two of them far away across the hill. Andrew knew he hadn't a chance now to get the sheep gathered up and penned within the time limit, so he walked out to help Lass drive them down off the course.

Sandy Big Alec wore a rumpled brown tweed coat and cap, and baggy knickers. He was leaning on a stout stick and talking with Piper Rory.

"Hasna been a decent run yet," he was saying, in his loud and gravelly voice. "Och, I've seen times at Rothiemore Trials when there wouldn't be a dog fail to pen the sheep!" He had a telescope slung on a strap over his right shoulder and Davie edged around to have a look at it. It was his old glass! He didn't buy the one at Buchanan's then, or if he had, he hadn't brought it out today in the rain.

"I see you're down to run Fly." It was Iain McLeod, Piper Rory's son.

"Aye. In the Novice Class. I don't know how he'll do."

"You'll have to bawl at him in this wind," said Iain.

"I'm hoping he'll do it all by himself. No matter how much shouting you do, it wouldn't carry that far."

"Jamie Grant has the best run up until now, I think. Or old man Gillis," said Iain, "but the best of them's still to come—after the Novice Class."

"I see Sandy Big Alec over there, talking with your dad. He's not got his dogs with him."

"Och no! He's won the Cup three times with Meg or Turk and now he can't compete at Rothiemore. But he's going to the Glenavon Trials next month, he says."

"I don't wish him any luck!" said Davie, looking at Sandy Big Alec.

"Och, nor I! Nor anybody! But he's got two good dogs there for all his bellowin' at them."

There was a burst of clapping and cries of "Good lad!" "That's it!" Mr. Cowan and his dog Nell had penned their sheep. It was much the best showing so far.

"And now," came from the megaphone, "we'll have the running of the Novice Class. There are five entries—all young dogs in their first competition—and they'll run in this order—Mr. Geordie Stewart with Floss, Robert Gillis with Glen, Mr. Cowan with Swan, Davie Matheson with Fly, and . . . . . . " But Davie never did hear who the last contestant was. His heart was thumping, and his hands were shaking so that the chain on Fly's leash rattled.

"Don't be afeard, Davie boy," said Father, clapping a hand on his shoulder. "If he does all right, he does all right and if he makes a botch of it . . . well, there's other dogs have done that this afternoon. Just do your best, and remember not to press the sheep too hard when you come down to getting them in the pen."

Davie was thinking he'd be happy enough if Fly would bring the sheep down so that he would get them *anywhere near* the pen.

Geordie Stewart had a bonnie looking collie, but she didn't seem to have much command of the sheep. She stood off a way and even barked at them, but they wouldn't move for her. And Robert Gillis wasn't much better with his Glen, who drove his sheep here and there all over the hill before getting them down near the pen. They didn't go through the gate either.

But Mr. Cowan's white pup seemed to know what she was about. She made a nice outrun to get around behind the sheep. Then she clapped down on the ground for a moment, just like an experienced old dog, before creeping forward to drive the sheep slowly down the hill. They missed the gate amid-field but Swan brought them down nicely all together to Mr. Cowan.

Davie was just beginning to think that he and Fly would have no chance at all against such a good young dog, when Mr. Cowan and the white pup began to have trouble. Now it was necessary to separate one of the sheep from the other four, and Davie well knew how difficult it was. Sheep like to stick together when you want to separate them, and when you want to hold them together they are determined to run off in every direction.

"If he can get past the shedding without too much trouble he'll win, I'm thinkin'," Davie heard someone say. "There'll be none of these young dogs get them into the pen."

But finally somehow, Mr. Cowan *did* get one sheep separated from the rest, and even though the ewes were frightened and nervous by then, he and Swan crowded them into the pen and banged shut the gate. There was a burst of clapping from the crowd.

"Aye, that's the winner! No doubt of it," exclaimed the voice behind Davie.

"The next contestant—Davie Matheson, with Fly!"

It felt very queer to be out there by the starting post all alone, with Fly beside him, and a hundred pairs of eyes all turned on him, watching. Davie squinted in the raw wind, watching for the men to drive *his* five sheep over the ridge and down to the flag. Oh, it was a long way off! Fly was more accustomed to the lower pasture, although Father and Davie had been taking him out on the hill with the older dogs lately and he had done well enough.

"Ay, there they come! See them, Fly? D'you see the sheep?" Davie pointed up to the top of the rocky hillside. Fly saw them all right.

"Ready!" said Captain MacPherson.

"Whssht, Fly! Get out away!" Davie sent Fly off on the run and from that time until the dog was back at his feet again he forgot all about the crowd behind him.

Fly ran out and up the hill very slowly, threading his way carefully among the rocks and heather. It seemed a long time before he came round behind the five black-faced sheep and crouched down for a moment so he wouldn't startle them into headlong flight.

"Ah, that's it!" Davie muttered to himself. There was no use shouting at Fly now. The dog would never hear with such a wind blowing across the hill. Suppose he just sat there, like Andrew's Lass had done! Suppose they turned out to be sticky, stubborn creatures!

But Fly edged forward and the sheep retreated down the hill. A nice steady lift! Good! Now the next thing was to try and get them through the gap—two hurdle gates set up near the bottom of the hill with a gap between them. That wouldn't be easy. Sheep have a notorious objection to going through any kind of gap. Anyway, they weren't heading in that direction.

Davie whistled and whistled, to bring Fly around to the left to head the sheep through the gap. He cupped his hands round his mouth and shouted his loudest "Come by! Come by!" Whether Fly heard him or whether he just used his own head for it when he saw the gate, the dog swung over to the left of the black-faced ewes and pressed them toward the opening. They didn't want to go through, but he made them.

"Oh Fly, Fly! Good dog!" Davie whispered to himself. Now he was within earshot and the two of them could work together, Davie and the dog.

Things had been going almost too well. Now suddenly their luck changed. The leader of the sheep stopped and would not budge. She turned and faced the dog. Fly crouched and looked her boldly in the eye, as though to say "Now, don't try any tricks!" Slowly Fly crept forward, and the ewe stamped her foot at him.

"Steady, Fly!" called Davie. "Come in, lad!"

It was the ewe that gave way, but she darted away and the others pounded after her. Fly was after them in a flash, but they were off on a wild break down a gully, and Davie's hopes fell crashing into the pit of his stomach.

They would be half way to Loch Strome before the young dog could turn them! But no! Fly was round and past them like the wind, and he drove them back across the gully and up to where Davie was standing. Och, a bonnie dog! He stood beyond them triumphant—master of those five stubborn, silly sheep.

Davie moved in now with his stick to shed one of the sheep, and separate it from the others. Now that they were frightened and panting it would be no easy thing to do.

Slowly, slowly Davie edged forward reaching his stick far out and tapping the ground like a blind man. The sheep were so jumpy that the slightest wrong move would send them off in a flurry.

"Now! This one, Fly!" Davie and Fly got one of the sheep away from the rest but couldn't keep her from going back to them. Well, no matter. The minutes were flying and there was a time limit.

Fly was all around the sheep, first on one side and then on the other, keeping them bunched together.

Now, to get them into the pen! Davie took the rope and swung the gate of the pen wide open, and reached his stick wide too. It seemed such a little pen, just six feet square. No wonder the sheep did not like to go into it, with all the free hills of Inverness around them.

The balky old ewe looked around for a possible way to escape. The gate and the boy were on one side and it seemed as if the pesky dog was everywhere else. She made a lunge to the right, but Fly was there like a shot and turned her into the pen. The others crowded in at her heels and Davie slammed the gate shut!

❋   ❋   ❋   ❋

Davie was trembling. He had been trembling ever since they had penned the sheep, he and Fly, and that was over an hour ago. He'd been clapped on the back by a dozen or more, and he'd been asked a lot of questions by Iain McLeod and the other boys, and he'd been hugged by Mum and the girls.

Father nodded his head. "You did well, Davie! Aye, you did well. It'll be close, mind ye, for Mr. Cowan had a good run with Swan, even though she didn't bring them through the gate. And he might have had them penned a bit faster maybe, though I'm not sure of it."

Yes, Davie was still trembling. Even when Father went out to the starting post with Moss, he couldn't fix his mind on it. Everything seemed to be in a sort of fog—a lovely, exciting fog!

"Hey there, young Matheson!"

It was Sandy Big Alec!

"Come here, lad! You've a fair to middling dog there." Sandy Big Alec's rough voice was saying. "Eager—though any young pup's eager. Aye, and I've seen them grow headstrong and useless before they're a year older."

"He's descended from Old Hemp, sir," said Davie.

"Old Hemp? Pfft! Huh, they say that about half the dogs in Scotland."

Davie said nothing. He wished Sandy Big Alec would turn away.

"I'll buy the dog from ye, gin you're wantin' to sell him," Sandy Big Alec went on. "Not that he's too promising as a Trials dog, but he'd do for the hill. A bit loose-eyed he is. And hasty, but I'd take that out of him in a hurry."

"I. . . . I can't sell him. He's not. . . . I want t' keep him!" Davie stammered.

"Come, come, now, lad! I'll offer a fair price—more than his promise is worth. And is he a bit blind in yon eye?"

"No, I . . . I'm keepin' him! . . . . Anyhow he's not mine to sell!"

"Hm! Not yours eh? Who does he belong to then?"

"He belongs to Old Billy Bayne sir, that's who. I'm just keeping him for Billy Bayne!"

"Well . . .! Well . . .!"

"Aye, Old Billy's sick and gone away to Perth."

Sandy Big Alec chewed on his fingernail. "To Perth, eh? . . . Well!" and with that he turned away and went over to the tea tent.

It was after five o'clock when the trials ended and the crowd gathered around the judges' table to hear the results.

Captain MacPherson gathered the score sheets and whispered and nodded with the other two judges.

"Well ladies and gentlemen," he said, "it's been a good meeting in spite of the weather. I'll not keep you, for it's getting late and there's more rain coming on. I'd like to announce the winners and congratulate them—congratulate you all on the way you're training your collies. The world's cleverest and most accomplished dog is the Border Collie, but he must be understood and properly trained; and as long as we've shepherds and handlers who are wise and patient with their dogs, we'll have good sheep dogs in our Scottish highlands. Now—

"Winner of the Shepherd's Trophy and a twelve pound prize of money, Mr. Neil MacKay of Dalwhinnie, with his dog Roy. And a close second with a cash prize of eight pounds Mr. Angus Matheson of Crubenbeg Farm, with Moss . . . .

"First prize in the Novice Class, five pounds in money and this beautiful shepherd's crook carved by Mr. Finlayson—the winner of this class is Davie Matheson with his young dog Fly! . . . . . . "

Davie's head swam, and he had a curious choked-up feeling in his throat, halfway between laughing and crying. He stumbled forward to take the envelope and Mr. Finlayson's crook. His hand was shaken by Captain MacPherson. He was very happy!

Chapter Six

ADVENTURE AND DISASTER

The rain and bad weather which began on the day of the Rothiemore Trials continued for more than a week. All the ditches were running with water. The rivulets and burns were in full spate and the waters of the Truim crashed and boiled down over the rocks below General Wade's bridge, and then flooded over the banks until the lower pasture looked like a lochan.

It was poor weather for the grouse shooting. The season opened on August the twelfth, and Lord Ennismuir brought a party of his friends from London and Edinburgh to the big Lodge. The Finlaysons were busy as could be, helping to get the house ready and stocked with food, and Mr. Finlayson had been hiring beaters in Rothiemore and the district around. The beaters spread out in a long straight line on the hill and walk forward waving their white flags to chase the grouse toward the shooting butts.

Davie and Iain went over several days, and even Morag went twice, and they all came home soaking wet. Beating is tiring sometimes.

"I don't mind the rain so much," said Morag, "but I don't like my feet being all soggy from sloshing through the heather."

"But you've money in your pockets for it, and you'll dry out overnight," laughed Father.

Lord Ennismuir and his friends got so sick of the rain they decided to go down to the Festival in Edinburgh for a few days. They set out in their cars on Thursday morning (though some of them took the morning train from Rothiemore station), and the very next day, Friday, the sun was shining and the air was clear as crystal. There were big ragged clouds still in the sky but they didn't carry rain.

Davie and Iain MacLeod had been planning on the first free day to climb up and see whether there were any young eagles in the nest high up on Craig Dhu. Not too near! Oh no, not with the old birds around! But if you climbed up the scree under the very top of Craig Dhu you could look over to the narrow ledge, where the eagles had built their eyrie of sticks and bracken.

"My dad says he'll put a shot in any eagle he sees, if he's handy to a gun," said Iain as they left the moor and started up the lower slope of Craig Dhu. Fly was along with them, and Iain's dog Jaff.

"But it isn't true that eagles carry off the lambs! Mr. Finlayson says so! And my father says it'd be a bad thing for the hill shepherds if there were no eagles around."

"Aye, but they *do* kill the lambs. Everyone says."

"Yes, yes, once or twice maybe, an eagle has taken a lamb. But all the more often it's taken a fox or a hoodie crow, and a hundred rabbits."

"Well, you'd better tell yon eagles to stay on your side of Craig Dhu then!" declared Iain, darkly.

"What did ye bring for lunch?" said Davie. In his own pocket were two hard-boiled eggs and some slabs of nice fresh bread.

"I didn't see what they put in—meat sandwiches, I guess. And I've got a pocket full of oat cakes. We can get water from a burn."

Davie stopped beside the dyke, where the old road to Inverness used to run. "Let's go round by the bothy. I haven't been there all this year."

"Aye, but we'll not go further round the hill. I've no wish to meet up with Sandy Big Alec!"

"Och, he'll not hurt you!" said Davie. "He's a dour and sulky man, that's all!"

Iain walked on ahead, swinging his stick at the heather. "My granny says he's got the Evil Eye. Last time he was at our place the milk soured."

"He was wanting to buy Fly at the Trials."

"Was he, now! How much did he offer you?"

"He didn't say for how much. I said he wasn't mine really, anyway!"

"What did you say that for!" cried Iain. "I'd have asked a big price!"

"I wouldn't sell Fly . . . . if he *were* my dog, . . . not even for a big price!"

They climbed up the rocky slope of Craig Dhu, following the sheep tracks through the purple heather, over the humps and ledges. The dogs trotted behind them or raced off on the scent of mountain hares. They could look down now all over Crubenbeg Farm and the valley of the Truim thick with pines and birches. There was Finlayson's house standing by itself and lonely, and farther over near the gamekeeper's house the byres and barns and sheepfold belonging to Lord Ennismuir. The big Lodge was out of sight at the head of the glen.

The heather was in full bloom now, colouring the hillside with its tiny purple flowers, and here and there in sheltered places the cow-berries were ripening in red clusters.

71

They were beginning to feel hungry when they came to the old ruined bothy. It was an old-time shepherd's cottage, but no one had lived there for years and years. The stone walls were standing almost as sound as ever, but the thick sod roof, and the poles which supported it had fallen in long ago. There was a sort of cave at one end of the hut under the fallen roof. The doorway opened into it and light came in through the small window space in the stone wall.

"Father shelters here sometimes in bad weather," said Davie, "but the sheep are seldom down this way on the hill."

They came to the stone dyke below the ruined cottage and stopped for breath, for it was a steep climb. The dogs continued scouting around for the scent of a fox or a hare.

"What's got into Fly?" said Iain. Fly had stopped stock still with one front paw raised and his nose pointing to the bothy.

"There's something *in* the old house—or somebody!" Davie said, and he gave a low whistle. He whistled again, and Fly trotted back beside him. Iain caught hold of Jaff's collar and the boys stood watching the open door of the old house.

Suddenly a man appeared in the doorway—a big man, a stranger they had never seen before around Rothiemore! The big man stepped outside the bothy and he was followed by a smaller man a little older and with stooped shoulders. They looked all around. Finally the stooped man caught sight of the boys beyond the dyke and the two men strode over toward them across the grass. Fly growled.

"Hey there!" shouted the burly, big one. His face wore a fierce frown. "What are you doin'? What are you pryin' around here for?"

"We just happened by," said Davie. "It's my father's farm, down at Crubenbeg, and this is part of our hill."

The two men looked at each other. The burly man started to say something and then stopped, biting his lip. Then he smiled, and the little man looked at him and smiled too.

"Och, sure! This is your hill, eh? Well now, we're just walking through, my friend and I . . . We've come over the top from Dalwhinnie." He turned and nodded at the older man.

"You don't keep many sheep at this end o' your hill, eh?"

"No, they seem to prefer it further down along," said Davie.

"Aye. And it's been a long time since the bothy's been used, eh? You don't come up here much, eh?"

"No, not often. It's the first since lambing time I've come by."

"Is it, now? Well now, we must be getting along, eh Harry? We're hiking down into Rothiemore and then over to the Cairngorms." The big man pulled out his watch, and snapped it open. "Aye, Harry. We must be on our way."

The other man just nodded—he hadn't said a word all the time—and they started off down the brae.

The boys watched them go, and Fly growled again. "That's queer!" Davie said, when the men were out of earshot. "I was thinking it might be the sheep stealers!"

"Och, they're just walkers!" said Iain. "There's been a lot of hikers around all summer—bird watching, or gathering mosses and stones and the like, or just plain walking for the pleasure of it!"

"Aye, but they don't look like regular hikers. They had no packs or maps."

"And they've no dogs with them, so it's not the sheep stealers! They couldn't gather up many sheep without a dog."

"You're right," Davie admitted. "I guess they're only walkers. But what were they so mad about, when they saw us?"

"Gave them a bit of a start, I guess. I thought it was Sandy Big Alec at first. Let's have a look in the bothy."

Iain peered in at the empty window and then stepped inside the door of the ruined cottage.

"It'd make a good hut for us—a secret meeting place. We could call it 'The Unknown' because practically no one comes here at all, or knows of it."

"It would be a bonnie place to keep a lookout. See! You can look all over our glen, right down to the Spey. You can see the Town Clock at Rothiemore, and if you had a good glass you could tell the time by it even!"

The dogs were nosing around the nooks and crannies of the ruined house. Davie stood out in front of the bothy while Iain prowled around inside. "We could bring a kettle and things up," Davie heard him say. "We could stay the night too if we mended the roof a bit."

"Iain!" Davie called. "Come out here! Look, you can see along *both* sides o' Craig Dhu from here, though not around as far as Sandy Big Alec's house. But there's Truim Barracks and there's the Great North Road."

"Aye," Davie went on, "if we were to keep a watch here, and had Fly with us, and a good glass . . . ! And Jaff too, of course! Aye, maybe then we'd catch the sheep stealers!"

"We'd better do it right soon then," said Iain, "or school will be starting. We've got but four weeks!"

"I wish I'd a glass of my own," Davie said, half to himself, " . . . . like the one in Buchanan's shop!"

They ate their lunches at the old bothy. Fly and Jaff didn't share it because they were fed only twice a day. Then they all—boys and dogs—stretched out on the grass in the warm sun for a short rest.

"There's one!" cried Iain. Davie opened his eyes with a start. He had been asleep, almost. "There's one o' the eagles! See, he's got something in his claws, a rabbit or something. They must have some young ones in the nest!"

They were rested now and it didn't take them very long to climb the rest of the way, and then scramble up the loose scree to a point where they could look across into the eyrie of the golden eagles.

"There's *two* young ones!" Davie said, peering across at the nest. "See! They're almost white, with dark speckles. It's hard to see them against the rock."

"I see them!" exclaimed Iain. "Look now there's the old un coming in. He's got a branch, is it, in his beak?"

"Aye, making the nest bigger. Mr. Finlayson says they do, when they've young eaglets in it. Och! I wish I'd a glass! I aim to *have* one

75

too, as soon as I've the money for it. I'm going to save every shilling I get as a beater at the grouse shooting."

They sat there for nearly an hour and watched the comings and goings of the parent birds. When both the old eagles were away the young ones seemed to be scuffling with each other.

"Just like bairns or puppies!" said Davie.

"Let's start back now. We'll follow the Truim down to the bridge. Then I'll have to be off home or I'll miss my tea." Iain hardly finished one meal when he began looking forward to the next. But he wasn't any fatter for it.

There were sheep from Crubenbeg Farm scattered here and there on the hill.

"See yon ewe with her two lambs?" said Davie. "Hold your Jaff now, and I'll have Fly bring them in here to me." He sent Fly away on the errand, and whistled him to hold back, to drive them round some rocks and across a narrow place in a rushing mountain burn. Fly went about it like a good servant, using his own wits and listening too for Davie's shouts and whistles.

"Aye, he does real good for a young un!" said Iain, full of admiration. "No wonder Sandy Big Alec wanted him! Now I'll try Jaff on the sheep in this corrie. See them all, Jaff? Go out away now!"

Jaff ran in a wide circle round the edge of the corrie and tried to gather up the ewes and their lambs, though it was not easy. He urged them together at last, but they were in danger of getting away on him, running down the hill. Then Davie sent Fly out to bring them round, and the two dogs together mustered them into a nervous huddle.

When they came to the stream they turned and followed it down the valley. It was a twisting line of dashing, foaming white water amid the lush green grass and purple heather, plunging now and again over an outcrop of dark rock.

"Here's where we nearly lost a heft of sheep last February in the

76

big blizzard," Davie said. "Thirty of them, all black-faced ewes, and most o' them within a week or two of lambing."

"Aye, it was blustery. I didn't get to school for a week!"

"Moss and Sweep found them all, under the snow, and Father dug them out. They missed one though, and it was there for five days before they went back and searched it out!"

Soon the stream was joined by another burn and by the time it reached the rolling moorland at the bottom of Craig Dhu, the Truim had grown to a real river.

Davie climbed on a flat rock and looked out over the moor.

"Hold up a minute!" Davie said. "Father put all those ewes and their lambs in the big pasture the day before yesterday. I'm sure he did! He told me when I came home from beating that he'd cleared them all off the moor!"

Iain joined him on the rock, and the dogs leaped up beside them.

"The gate's open in the dyke. Someone's been through it, or the sheep have pushed a pole down."

"I should get them back in . . . or they'll be all over the hill. Here Fly! Bring them here to me lad." Fly and Jaff were happy to obey. Iain hurried over to the left to head them down the hill, and they began to collect the straying sheep.

Davie whistled from time to time and the sheep came trotting in without difficulty. Jaff did his part well enough though he was inclined to drive the lambs too fast. When they were nearly at the gate in the dyke, Davie missed Fly. He was nowhere to be seen. Davie whistled and called but the dog did not come.

"That's strange!" he thought. If it had happened three months ago, he would have expected it and been cross with the puppy; and he would have finished the job himself and walked on home. But now . . .

"Will you take them in!" he called to Iain. "I've got to see what's come over Fly!"

Davie went all the way back to the Truim, calling and whistling along the way. There was no sign of Fly. Yet the dog had certainly been over there after a heft of sheep. Davie walked downstream for fifty yards beside the white water. Then almost at General Wade's bridge he saw the dog——!

Fly was crouched on a rock beside a swirling backwater of the swollen river, and his teeth were locked tight on the wool of a frightened ewe which had fallen into the water. Davie scrambled down the bank to help. He grabbed the forelegs of the sheep and pulled her up to safety on the rock.

"Ah Fly! You knew I'd come!" He put his arms around the collie's neck and hugged him against his chest. "You couldn't come when I called, but you knew I'd be along! Och, you're a bonnie dog! You'll be a grand dog for the hill!"

Davie and Fly ran the rest of the way up the rough road after leaving Iain at the bridge. Tea would be waiting and Fly was going to have a tasty supper and a lot of praise and petting. Maybe now even Aunt Flora would admit he was no common dog!

But there outside the kitchen door was Father—talking with Sandy Big Alec!

"Davie, lad," Father said slowly, "Mr. MacMurchie's here to get Fly. He's bought your wee dog!"

It was as though Davie had been struck down by a bolt of lightning! No! No, it couldn't be!

"He can't! He can't have him!" Davie cried. "He's not our dog to sell! He belongs to old Billy!"

"Yes, yes, now Davie!" said Father. "But Mr. MacMurchie has been to Perth and found where old Billy was . . . . He's got a paper from old Billy showing he's paid for the dog. Here, look . . . . !"

Davie's head was whirling. He just stood there with his lips trembling, looking first at Father and then at Sandy Big Alec. He felt as though he couldn't breathe, he couldn't move or say a word.

Sandy Big Alec's fat red face had a sly smile on it, and he fingered the leash he'd brought to take Fly home.

Davie turned and ran into the house, through the kitchen, and upstairs to his own room. He slammed the door and flung himself on the bed, and began to sob as though his heart would break.

Chapter Seven

DAY OF EXCITEMENT

If Davie had had much time to think about it during the next couple of weeks he would have been sick with unhappiness. As it was, he stumbled around only half alive. His heart lay in his chest like a heavy lump, and sometimes he had to turn away from Morag or Father or Mr. Finlayson so they wouldn't see the tears welling up in his eyes. It did not seem possible that there was no Fly waiting at the door for him, no dog at his heel, no companion if he walked out on the moor or climbed down the glen among the rocks by Truim Falls, no helper if he went on a message for Mum. He was lonely.

He just couldn't let himself think about Fly being over there at Sandy Big Alec's, on the other side of Craig Dhu. Sandy Big Alec was rough and loudmouthed. To get the best results with Fly, you had to be gentle and quiet with him and let him know that you were counting on him to do the job well. Sandy Big Alec didn't know how to be gentle.

So it was a good thing they were busy at Crubenbeg Farm. All the sheep and lambs had to be gathered from the hill—a thousand of them, if they found them all—and brought down to the fold for the dipping. Mr. Finlayson came over, and Piper Rory and some of the other men from round about, to help with the gathering of the sheep on the mountain and the many jobs there were to do at the fold. Mrs. Finlayson and Annie came too, to help Mum in the kitchen. For at dipping time and at shearing time, the kitchen was always full of food—stacks of homemade bread and cakes and jam tarts, and the good smell of roast beef all through the house.

There were cups of tea ready at all hours, and the two big black pots of porridge simmering on the stove for the men's breakfast.

Davie had helped Father and Piper Rory gather the farthest slopes and corries of Craig Dhu before the other men arrived so there would be no time lost. Moss and Sweep knew that it was a big occasion and they worked valiantly, without ever seeming too tired and footsore to dash away another half mile to bring in a couple of straying ewes or a ba-a-ing lamb which had lost its mother. Piper Rory's dogs worked hard too, Jaff and Luck; but Davie couldn't help but think how well Fly would have taken his part in the gathering, full of spirit and energy and eager to outrun a heft of sheep or another dog.

"We're in luck," said Father, scanning the sky. "It'll not rain tomorrow." If it rained, the dipping was put off, for the wet wool of the sheep wouldn't soak up much of the yellow dip.

Callum Campbell came out to Crubenbeg, for he was the policeman and since it was the law to dip all sheep twice in the year, he had to see that it was done. Putting the sheep through the bath prevented the spread of disease among the highland flocks.

"Now you and Geordie Frazer should be off hunting for the sheep-stealers instead of bothering us poor law-abiding crofters," Piper Rory called out. The men joked with Callum Campbell, and at dinner time some of them tried on his policeman's hat to see how they looked in it.

The dipping bath was about twenty feet long, filled with yellow liquid, and in the air was the strong, clean smell of it. The sheep were no more anxious to take their bath than a small boy on Saturday night. The men took turns at the different jobs—sorting out the four-year-olds and wether lambs, sliding the sheep into the bath, ducking them under, and gathering them into the pens after the work was done. Piper Rory, who was boisterous and lively, took first turn at the hardest job, tumbling the struggling sheep into the water. Davie helped Mr. Finlay-son mix up the dip, and then went down to lend a hand with penning the yellow-coloured sheep after they had come up out of the trough. They were bleating and unhappy.

Ah, but it was hard work for everyone—a full day, a crowded day, that made Davie drop off to sleep that night as soon as his head hit the pillow.

Next morning Davie slept very late. It was just as well perhaps, for Fly had come back in the night, and Father had taken him over again to Sandy Big Alec's, before Davie woke up.

"Poor wee dog!" Mum said. "He's not used to it yet, over yon, all among strangers and no children there to play with when the day's work is done."

"Och, it's a shame to take him back like that!" scolded Aunt Flora. "And I hope Angus has a word or two to say to that big scoundrel when he hands the dog over."

"Why?" asked Davie. "Was something wrong? Is Fly all right?"

"Wrong? Aye, there was! He'd been beaten and run away, that's what!"

"Now Flora, that's only guesswork," Mum said, sliding some bacon onto Davie's plate. "Father only said the dog *may* have had a bruise on him. He couldn't say for sure . . . . . He *might* have had, for Sandy Big Alec's not above giving a dog a whack, if it doesn't obey him."

"Father shouldna have taken him away until I came down," Davie said.

"Oh, I think it was best that he did, Davie," said Mum, and patted him on the shoulder.

"We're going to the trials at Glenavon on Saturday, Davie," Father announced one day. "Och, it's hard work at sheep dipping time helping out at the different farms, and we need a wee break from it."

"Are we all going?" cried Morag. "Can't we go too?"

"Not this time. Just me an' Davie this time. Mr. Fleming's going to take us in his car. Three people and two dogs will be tight enough in Mr. Fleming's little car."

"Two dogs?" Davie said. "Mr. Fleming's just got one dog."

Father rubbed his chin and cleared his throat. "Well . . . I thought I'd run Moss in the Trials. He's come along well this year—mostly because he was spurred on by Fly. Oh, he's not ready for Glenavon yet, likely, but it'll do no harm to run him in company with some of the best sheep dogs in the North."

"Aye, and in the South too," Davie added, "for there's going to be dogs there from Ayr and from Argyl."

The day of the Sheep Dog Trials at Glenavon was very different from the squalls and gales of Trials Day at Rothiemore. A pleasant September day it was, warm and clear, with only a light breeze blowing down the valley.

Davie rode in the back seat between the two dogs, noting all the cottages and crofts and hirsels along the way, and half-listening to the talk of Father and Mr. Fleming up in front. It was not until they went through Glenavon and came over a hill suddenly upon Caulmore Farm that he felt a wave of excitement. Here before them was the setting for the Trials and the crowds gathering for the great event.

This was different from the Rothiemore Trials. There were men at the ticket gates, and the cars were parked in an L-shaped pattern behind the crowd. Two big marquee tents had been set up, one for the secretary and officials, and one for tea and refreshments. Here, the competitors were announced over booming loud speakers. Och yes! Beside these Glenavon Trials the ones at Rothiemore were very small indeed. Davie was glad that *he* did not have to walk out in front of that crowd and run a dog!

There were several hundred people there already, and more coming

all the time. There were many shepherds and crofters and their families of course, but there were townspeople too, in clothes of a different cut, and a number of the men were wearing the kilt. Some of them were quite elegant.

Out in front, beyond the judges table and the rope, the Trials course was laid out on rough, uneven meadow land. There was a marshy part running across the middle, beyond which the land sloped uphill to the flag where the five sheep were set out for each competitor. On the other side of the hill was a loch, or maybe it was an inlet of the sea— Davie wasn't sure—and the waters of the loch were like silver shining bright. There were mountains around, all dark, purple and green. The real faraway ones were flat blue against the sky.

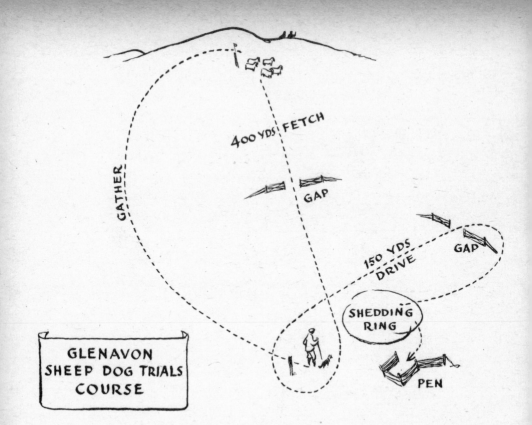

400 YDS FETCH

GATHER

GAP

150 YDS DRIVE

GAP

SHEDDING RING

PEN

GLENAVON
SHEEP DOG TRIALS
COURSE

"It's a long fetch down the hill. About four hundred yards, wouldn't you say?" said Mr. Fleming, eyeing the layout of the Trials course.

"Aye," agreed Father. "And there's a chance o' trouble if the dog drives his sheep into yon marsh."

"Aye, it would be well to keep clear of the marsh. Well now, let's get a program."

Mr. Fleming bought three programs. "You'll want one too, Davie," he said, "and they're but sixpence."

There were the prizes. "Twenty-five pounds!" Davie whistled.

"Very good, isn't it, Davie? It wouldn't be bad at all, to go home with twenty-five pounds as first prize . . . . . and the Cup!"

"Championship Cup, by Glenavon Agricultural Society; Special

Prizes . . . . " Davie read out. Then he turned the page to look at the list of competitors.

1.	James Cameron, Tillyloch	"Queen"
2.	A. J. Fraser, Inverness	"Wag"
3.	Robert Gibson, Balcorrie	"Shep"
4.	Duncan Stewart, Largie, Ayrshire	"Rye"
5.	Duncan Stewart, Largie, Ayrshire	"Spot"

"He's one o' the best, Duncan Stewart" Davie said to himself. "Aye, and A. J. Fraser's 'Wag' took second prize last year." He read on down the page—

14.	A. Fleming, Rothiemore	"Chip"
	. . . .	
	. . . .	
17.	Angus Matheson, Crubenbeg	"Moss"
	. . . .	
	. . . .	
23.	Alec MacMurchie, Rothiemore	"Turk"
24.	Alec MacMurchie, Rothiemore	"Fly"

That was Sandy Big Alec! And he was going to run Fly here in the Glenavon Trials!

Davie wandered up and down through the crowd, but he didn't see Sandy Big Alec anywhere. He had noticed several of the dogs chained to the fence posts along the road waiting their turn, so he went back there to see if Fly were among them. The dogs were restless, not because they minded being chained up, but they were impatient and they were wondering how the other dogs were getting on, beyond the crowd. But Fly wasn't anywhere along the fence.

Davie went up and sat beside Father while Mr. Fleming was running Chip. Chip made a nice run out after his sheep and lifted them gently before starting down the hill.

"He's doing good so far," Father said, "but Mr. Fleming had better bring his dog around or he'll have the sheep into the marsh. Och, he's got them on the run now . . . . Fah! They're into the marsh and it'll not be easy to get them back and through the gate!"

Mr. Fleming did his best but he had to bring the five sheep down without going through the gate. That meant he didn't have a very good chance for high marks unless all the rest was done perfectly. Then Chip began to have more trouble with one of the ewes which was wild and balky.

"Davie! Look!" Father whispered, and his voice was agitated. "Doesn't that look like one of our ewes—one of those the sheep stealers took in the Spring?"

Davie did not know their sheep the way Father did, and he wondered how on earth Father could tell them apart.

"Och, I'm probably all wrong about it, but nevertheless I'm going over to the pen and see for myself when Mr. Fleming brings them in. Here Davie, you take Moss. I'll be right back!"

Sheepstealers would sometimes disfigure the ear marks on lambs, or change the brands on the horns of old sheep and then take them away somewhere to a distant market to sell. If Father found that the brand marks had been changed, he might be able to trace the sheep-stealers! It would mean a lot to them all.

Davie sat by the rope with Moss and watched the next two competitors run their dogs. Each time he planned to himself how he would run the dog if it were his. It was easy to see someone else's mistakes, and to see the faults of the dog. Aye, but it took a cool head if you were up there yourself!

"The next competitor will be Mr. Angus Matheson, with Moss!" blared the loudspeaker.

Davie jumped to his feet and looked around wildly. He ran back to the edge of the crowd. He shouted. Nobody answered, but everyone looked at him. Father was nowhere to be seen.

Davie did not know what to do. He looked down at Moss. Then he slipped under the rope and ran across to the judges' table.

"He's gone somewhere . . . Mr. Matheson, my father. Maybe if you'll announce it again he'll hear."

So the loudspeaker blared out again. "Next competitor, Mr. Angus Matheson! Will Mr. Matheson report to the judges at once!"

They waited a minute—it seemed like half an hour—but Father did not come.

The judges shook their heads. "I guess we'll just have to cross it out!" said one of them.

Davie felt he had to do *something!* He couldn't just stand there and let it be crossed out, and let old Moss down, after coming so far for the Trials!

"Could I . . . could I run the dog for him?" he sputtered finally.

"Yes. Yes, if you want to. You're his son. But we'll have to hurry along!"

Davie ducked under the rope again and hurried out to the starting post, with Moss at his heels. The sheep were already out, up there on the hill by the flag.

"D'ye see them, Moss? Whssht! Go out away then!" And Moss raced out in a wide arc, climbing the rough slope of the hill.

Afterwards, it always seemed like a dream to Davie, but he heard all about it often enough from people who had been there and watched. Fancy! Him, Davie Matheson, running a dog at Glenavon Trials! Why he didn't even have a stick with him, until someone came out and put one in his hand!

Moss ran in a wide arc, clapped down, and then lifted the sheep and started down the brae. Davie remembered about the marsh and whistled Moss around to the left of them so they would keep clear of it. There was a little hesitation before Moss could urge them through the gate, but not enough to matter. The dog brought them down to Davie and around him in a tight little bundle, and drove them out again to go through the second gate.

But here things began to go wrong. One of the ewes felt they had been driven far enough now by this bossy black dog, and she led the others first to one side and then the other. She was determined not to go through that gate! Moss edged them up closer and then rushed in to try and push them through. . . . And he managed to send four of them into the gap. But the stubborn old ewe raced out to the side and joined the others near the marsh.

How Davie got the sheep separated at the shedding, and finally into the pen he never knew. But somehow he did, and slammed the gate shut, just a second or two after one of the judges called "Time!" They hadn't made it! Not quite. But Moss had behaved himself well, and there was nothing they need be ashamed of in the performance, either Davie or the dog!

Here was Father at last, waiting to help him take the five sheep over to the gathering pen. Mr. Fleming was there too.

"Davie lad, you did wonderful well! Aye, I'm proud of you! And Moss too, you're a bonnie dog!"

"Aye Davie, we saw the last bit," said Mr. Fleming. "I think you'd have been in for a prize if only you'd penned a bit quicker! But no mind! You made a good run of it."

"He did that!" laughed Father. "I couldn't have done it nearly so well myself!"

"I didn't know what t' do, when you weren't back," Davie said.

"Och lad, I'm sorry! We were looking over the sheep and I wasna thinking of anything else!"

"Was it one of ours, the ewe?" asked Davie.

"Yes, I'm sure of it. Though the mark on her's been changed. She

was sold to the farmer here, at a sale way down in Perth, but we might
be able now to trace the sheepstealers!"

They went over to the refreshment tent to get a cup of tea. The tea
tasted hot and good after all that excitement. Davie bought a bun too,
and a bar of chocolate; and even Moss had a tasty snack, which Father
had brought along.

Davie put the bar of chocolate in his pocket and wandered around
beside the tent, sipping the hot tea. He heard a low whine. There, tied
to a tent stake, was Fly!

In a moment Davie was down beside the wee dog, with his arms
around Fly's neck, and Fly's cold nose against his cheek. The dog was
squirming and wriggling in sheer delight.

"Oh Fly, Fly! It's good to see you" said Davie softly. "Have y' been
a good dog, now? I've missed you! I've missed you!"

He patted the dog's side and rubbed his back. There did not seem to be any bruises or tender places on Fly now. He was still thin but all good working collies are lean and bony.

It would be wonderful to have a dog like Fly all your own, thought Davie—that you had trained yourself and knew the sort he was! A dog who understood what you had in mind, and would do anything at all for you, in winter storms or at lambing time or gathering on the hill. A shepherd wouldn't be much good without his dog, and if the dog were one like Fly now . . . . .

"Here boy! Give us the dog!" It was Sandy Big Alec, bending over them and reaching for the tie chain!

"Let go the creature, boy! We're next on Trials course!" Sandy Big Alec's voice was like a biting raw wind, reaching right through to Davie's heart. Fly cringed down against the ground until Sandy Big Alec jerked him along by the chain.

Davie said nothing, but he felt sick, seeing the poor wee dog trotting along after the man. Fly's tail was drooping and his head hung down, like a dog with no spirit left at all.

When they had disappeared into the crowd, Davie took the cup back to the tea tent, and hurried off to find a good place beside the course.

The last competitor had just penned his sheep, and the loudspeaker droned out—"Mr. Alec MacMurchie, and Fly!"

Sandy Big Alec shuffled out to the starting post, still keeping Fly on the chain. They had to wait a minute or two for the sheep to be put out, up on the hill. The big man in his rumpled tweed clothes looked friendless somehow out there by himself. Davie did not feel any hatred for Sandy Big Alec, for all his harsh talk, for all that he might have beaten Fly. Fly was his dog, and he had got him fair enough. He had bought him from old Billy, honest and open. Davie felt rather sorry for the clumsy big man whom nobody liked, and who didn't really know how to be pleasant with his fellow creatures, men or dogs. But he wasn't a sheep stealer, Sandy Big Alec, no matter what Mr. Finlayson or anyone might think!

"Get out away, Fly! Whisht!" Sandy Big Alec slipped the clasp from Fly's collar and with a wave of his stick sent the dog out for the sheep.

Fly ran out in a long curving line, just right. He stopped, just right, to let the sheep get used to him. Then he lifted them carefully and brought them down the hill, swinging to the left and to the right to keep them on the move and headed straight for Sandy Big Alec. He didn't hurry them; nor did he let them dawdle—just right.

Davie could hear the men around him admiring the dog's work.

"Aye, there's a likely dog for ye! An' little more than a pup!"

"MacMurchie's luckier than he deserves! He bought the dog from an old tramp."

"Yon dog's the best yet! He'll have no nonsense from the sheep!"

"Och, too much fuss! Why doesn't he leave the dog alone?"

Now that Fly had the sheep down within shouting distance, Sandy Big Alec was roaring and bawling his orders, certain that he knew better than the dog what to do.

"Take time! Take time! Come round, come round now! Come round, I tell ye!"

Fly brought the five sheep through the first gate and swung them round behind Sandy Big Alec. He was doing a thorough job, but he seemed to be bustled and bothered by Sandy Big Alec's harsh bellowings. He drove them out now and through the second gap as neatly as though it were a fenced lane from which they could not escape.

Now for the shedding! Sandy Big Alec strode forward to separate one sheep from the rest. One of the ewes had a blue ribbon tied to her horn. She was the one to be shed and held away from the rest. It was always ticklish work, that needed gentle, careful handling.

"Och, the man's too hasty!" someone said. "He'll undo all the dog's work if he's not careful!"

Sandy Big Alec edged the sheep this way and that, while Fly held them steady. Fly lay full length on the ground, not a muscle moving, but his eyes blazing. One of the ewes made a move to the right, and in a flash Fly was up and had her back in line.

"This one!" shouted Sandy Big Alec, and thrust his stick between the sheep. Fly dashed in and the ewe was driven away from her companions and held away, ba-a-ing her protests to all the world.

"Aye, he's got it! Now to get them penned!"

"He's far out in front. He'll take the cup for certain sure!"

". . . if he gets them in the pen!"

"Och, he'll do that!"

The sheep were nervous. Now they needed just the right touch to get them penned. Too much forcing now would make them frantic and rebellious, and there would be no end of trouble urging them into the little pen.

Sandy Big Alec grasped the rope and swung the gate of the pen wide open.

"Come round, Fly! Come behind!"

Fly forced the sheep toward the pen gate. Sandy Big Alec was as jumpy and excited as the sheep now, for he knew that First Prize was right within his grasp! The Championship Cup and Twenty-five pounds! In another few minutes it might be his!

"Come in, Fly!" he yelled.

The wild ewe made a dash for it—off across the meadow at full speed. Fly was after her at once, and Sandy Big Alec was bawling and shouting after them, and trying to keep the other four sheep under control at the same time.

"Bring her round, bring her round, Fly! Come round, you muckle headed beast!

"Fly! Fly! What are you doin' with her, you stupid dog! Bring her in, bring her in!"

Fly brought the ewe round at last and drove her back to join the others. By now Sandy Big Alec was shaking with anger and excitement. The Cup! The Cup! There it was! So near and yet so far!

Sandy Big Alec reached out wide from the gate and waved his stick around, and yelled at Fly to drive the sheep into the pen. Fly kept close to the sheep trying to guard all sides of them at once. When he ran around to keep them from breaking past Sandy Big Alec's stick, the big man lost his head completely and whacked at the dog with his stick.

"Go round, go round! You no good mongrel, you! If I had y' by the scruff o' the neck, I'd knock the liver out of you!"

Fly held the sheep there, but he was afraid now to bring them up past the angry farmer. He hung back, and the five sheep stood still, at the mouth of the pen, and not all of Sandy Big Alec's shouts and threats could bring them into the enclosure.

Some of the men in the crowd began to laugh. Davie's hands were clenched so that his fingernails bit into his palms. He was trembling and crying to himself.

"That's not the way to treat a dog! That's not the way to make Fly do your bidding!" He thrust his clenched fists against his eyes, and the hot tears ran down his cheeks.

"Time! That'll do!" called the judge, and the sheep were still not in the pen. Sandy Big Alec slammed the gate shut angrily and threw his stick at the wee dog. But Davie didn't see it because his fists were tight against his tears.

A chill wind sprang up before the Glenavon Trials ended and the sun was sinking down behind clouds over the blue mountains. It was getting on toward six o'clock. Sandy Big Alec had left Caulmore Farm and taken his dogs with him.

Seven or eight more competitors had run their collies, after Sandy Big Alec, and now the prizes were being given out. Davie drifted dejectedly among the crowd but he could not summon up any further interest in the Trials. Finally he wandered over to Mr. Fleming's car and sat down beside Moss and Chip on the grass. He wasn't even curious about the winners. His ears were deaf to the speeches and announcements.

It was here that Father found him. "Davie! Davie! Come on over now! Quickly! You've won a prize! They've given you one of the Special Prizes!" He pulled Davie to his feet and propelled him through the crowd to the Officials' tent. On a table in front of it the Cups and things were spread out and the judge was handing out the money prizes.

"Here's Davie Matheson!" said Father, and pushed Davie forward into the circle.

"Davie Matheson. Ah yes! A Special Award for a young competitor giving an outstanding performance, together with a money prize of three pounds." The judge took off his glasses and looked down at Davie. "Let me shake your hand, lad; you ran the dog sensibly and well—especially as it was on the spur of the moment——. I expect we shall see a good deal more of you in our Scottish sheep dog trials in the future! Here, lad, is the money prize, and here is your Special Award!"

It was the telescope! . . . . *The telescope!* . . . . the bonnie glass which had been in Mr. Buchanan's shop window in Rothiemore!

Davie tried to smile, but somehow he couldn't. He was terribly pleased, excited, but at the same time his heart felt like a heavy stone. He mumbled his thanks and took the money and the telescope, then quickly turned away and squirmed through the crowd.

Chapter Eight

THE SHEEP STEALERS

After the Glenavon trials they settled down to a more regular life on Crubenbeg Farm—Davie and Morag getting ready to go back to school, and Christie with them this year, and Mum bustling around, bottling the wild fruit and storing away things for the winter. Father was always busy with something it seemed, for each season on a high-land sheep farm brings its own work.

From March onward one thing crowds close upon the heels of the next. Sometimes Father was worried or so tired he fell into bed right after supper. And sometimes he sat down in the evening, relieved and content—proud that he and the dogs had overcome difficulties on the rough and rocky hill farm.

First, it's the lambing season when one must be out on the hill a long, long day, caring for the new lambs and their mothers. Davie went out with Father whenever he could at lambing time. When a lamb died, they had to take the skin from the dead lamb and put it on another poor wee one who had lost its mother, and then try to persuade the old ewe that this one, in the borrowed coat, was really her own. She would sniff and sniff at it for a long while, but usually she would decide that it *must* be her own lamb, after all.

Then all through the spring and summer there was the endless war against foxes and hoodie crows and wildcats. Andrew Douglas was a great help with that. There had been no wildcats around Crubenbeg for two years since Andrew had shot the big one up on Craig Dhu.

"Aye, but there's sheep stealers now," said Andrew, "and they've taken more lambs than the wildcat!"

Next to the spring, Davie liked September best. Now in September came the sales—the Sheep Sales and the Ram Sales. When the sheep were gathered down from the hill for dipping, Father and Mr. Finlayson had sorted out the four year old ewes and wether lambs, and a few of the old rams, which they wanted to sell. They had to be sorted out in lots of twenty, and carefully sorted too, so as to bring the best price. Last year Davie had gone down to Perth with them. He was learning how to look in the mouths of the sheep to tell their age, and to tell how healthy they were by the whites of their eyes. He would pick out what he thought were the best ewes, and see whether Father and Mr. Finlayson agreed.

"Och Davie, you did not look well at yon sheep," said Mr. Finlayson. "You must look at her hoofs too, for signs of foot rot."

Yes, the autumn was a busy time, but it had a good sort of feeling to it, as though they were coming to the end of a job well done.

Quite early one morning, Davie was awakened by a noise at the back

door, beneath his window. There was an early morning mistiness in the air, the kind that rises in the glens and hollows on autumn nights. He lay there and listened for a minute and then he heard it again—a dog whining and scratching at the door. It was Fly!

Davie called out the window to the dog, and Fly ran off at once and disappeared. In a minute he was back again, whining as before. There was something wrong!

Father had been awakened too, either by Fly's whining or Davie's calling to the dog.

"It's Fly, come back," said Davie, "and he's acting queer and troubled."

"We'll see then!" said Father. "Put some clothes on, and your boots—and don't make a noise so's not to waken the others."

Within three minutes Davie was dressed and downstairs, and Fly was giving him a wagging, whimpering greeting at the kitchen door. Father was not far behind.

"Look!" cried Davie. "Look at Fly's back . . . .! There's blood on it! There's a cut . . . "

"Aye, there's a cut," said Father. "It looks as though he's been given a whack on it, with a heavy stick!"

Fly wriggled free and darted off through the birch and alder trees which sheltered the back of the house from the winds off Craig Dhu. He returned, as he had done before, and stood waiting, whining, urging them to follow.

Davie reached the open moor first and just beyond the trees he found a nervous huddle of sheep.

"They're ours!" exclaimed Father. "Some of our young ewes they are, off the hill!" He and Davie looked at each other and Father gave a low whistle. "It's the sheep stealers!" he said darkly.

They drove the frightened ewes into a pen in the fold and Davie closed the gate behind them.

"D'you think . . . ?" he began.

"Aye, that's it!" Father said, with a grim and determined look in his eyes. "It must be Sandy Big Alec! . . . He's been gathering them up there on Craig Dhu with Fly and his dogs, and Fly has brought some of ours away and got clouted for his pains!

"We've no time to lose, Davie," he said, "but first the wee dog's bruise has to be seen to, or he'll be stiff and sore from it."

The sun was rising when they started up the hill with Fly and Moss after the sheep stealers.

"It *must* be him! I cannot see how it would be anyone else, with Fly coming back to us like that," Father said. "Taking some of his own sheep too, to throw suspicion elsewhere."

"I feel kind of sorry for Sandy Big Alec," said Davie, panting as they hurried up the steep slope of the hill. "For all his being a dour man, and bawling at his dogs and other people too, he must be awful lonely with no one wanting to talk to him, and nobody to say a good word for him."

"No, he's not a happy man," Father agreed, "and it'll go hard for him if he's found to be stealing sheep."

"Are you going onto his land?" asked Davie.

"Aye and down to his house too, if we don't find him before!"

But when they came to the old bothy, Fly would go no farther. He hung back and whimpered, and refused to go along in spite of their coaxing.

"Ah, he's afraid of another clout from Sandy Big Alec," said Father. "Well, we'll just have to go on without him."

"Maybe he's wanting us to turn off here, and go down the brae."

"It *does* look like that," agreed Father.

"Off toward Truim! It's Truim Barracks he wants to go to!" cried Davie. "Remember? Old Billy said—'better have a look around Truim Barracks'!"

"Hsst! Maybe you're right! Aye, Sandy Big Alec wouldn't wish t' take the sheep home with him, for fear of being caught with them in his own fold. So he drives them down to Truim Barracks. He could easily pen them up there in one of the cellars, and come back and lift them when he chose—in the dark of the night even!"

Truim Barracks was a little over a mile from the old bothy. They made plans as they hurried along.

"If Sandy Big Alec's there by himself with the sheep, it'll not be difficult." Father whistled to the dogs to stay close at heel. "But it's more than likely he's got someone else in the crafty business with him—someone to help him change the horn markings and get the sheep off to the market.

"We'd best try and creep up quietly; we don't want any trouble."

"If they're there," said Davie, "I'll slip away to Rothiemore an' fetch Callum Campbell."

They made their way around to the back of Truim Barracks and scuttled across the open moor hoping they wouldn't be seen. Once they reached the high bare walls of the ruined stronghold they could breathe easier. The dogs were well trained and kept close beside them, making no sound, but Davie could see that Fly was getting stiff from the blow on his back.

They crept along until they came to an opening in the wall, and cautiously peered into the ruins. They could see no one, nor were there any sheep in the great centre square of the stronghold. Silently they crept around it searching in the smaller courts and crannies.

"Here they are Davie!" Father whispered excitedly. Sure enough, in one of the old cellars of the castle was a great heft of sheep. There must have been nearly sixty. The old cellar was partly a cave, partly open where the stone floor above it had fallen in, and it was barred up at the entrance to make a secure fold for the sheep.

"Even if tourists did come to Truim, it's not likely they'd notice them down here in this vault." Father and Davie looked all around the barracks, but there was no one about. Then Father climbed over the stones into the cellar and began examining the horns of the ewes. "Some of ours, and some of Piper Rory's, and a few of Sandy Big Alec's!" he announced.

"He must have gone off home" said Davie, "and what'll he do now that Fly's run away from him with those Crubenbeg sheep?"

"It's hard to say," Father said thoughtfully. "They might come back right away because of it, to get the marks changed and the sheep out of the district. But it's more likely they'll wait until dark. We'll have to lie quiet here and see."

"If it's going to be all day and into the night maybe, we'll have to have some food with us. And we'll have to let Mum know or she'll be wondering."

"Aye, you're right, Davie. I'll stay an' keep watch then, with the dogs. You be off now, and tell Mum what we're up to and maybe Morag can run in to Rothiemore and ask Callum Campbell t' join us."

Davie started off and then halted. "Should I take Fly?" he said.

"Aye, perhaps it'd be better if you took the wee dog home with you. Mother'll bathe the cut."

When Davie burst into the kitchen at Crubenbeg, the womenfolk were all up and finished with breakfast, and beginning to worry about Davie and Father.

"I couldn't think what would have taken you out of the house so early without a word to us about it," Mum said. "Here, Davie, have some porridge now, while I put some eggs on to boil hard. I'll fill a knapsack with bread and cheese and things. Will you be needing a jug of water?"

"No, there's a burn right handy. Put in a jug though, for us to have by us."

"Morag will be away to Rothiemore as soon as she's changed her boots. Goodness I'll be worried until the thing's over and you're both back here at Crubenbeg!"

Aunt Flora was boiling over with anger. "Och, that dour black-hearted lout of a Sandy Big Alec MacMurchie! It'll serve him right to get caught. Miserly with his own coppers he is, and not even content with that!"

107

"We're not sure of it yet," protested Davie, "but by the looks of it, it cannot be anyone else. I was half hoping it wouldn't be Sandy Big Alec somehow."

Morag came clattering down the stairs. "I've my heavy boots on. Now what am I to say to Callum Campbell?"

"Tell him to come right out to Truim Barracks and to bring Geordie with him. Better tell him about bringing some food, for it'll likely be at night when the sheep stealers come back." Davie thought for a minute. "I think you'd better tell them to hide themselves by the Great

North Road, where the lane turns in from it to Truim Barracks. Then there'll be no chance of the sheep stealers getting away!"

"I don't like the business," said Mum, as she closed the door behind Morag. "I don't like it at all; but he's got to be caught, there's no two ways about it!"

"I'll take my glass," said Davie, and went to the hall where it was hanging—the beautiful glass he had won at the Glenavon Trials. He had felt so badly that night after seeing Fly, and the botch Sandy Big Alec had made of handling the dog, that he came home and hung it there in the hall, and sat down to a supper he didn't feel like eating. He hadn't used the glass at all.

"Aye, take your glass, Davie," Mum said. "Then you'll be able to keep a sharp eye out for the thieves!"

Just then there was a knock at the door. Christie opened it, and Iain MacLeod pushed in, his eyes wild and his hair every which way under his cap. Behind him was Piper Rory.

"We met Morag at the bridge," gasped Iain. "She told us . . . !"

"Aye, she told us. . . We were just comin' over to ask for help with gatherin' our sheep. But now it looks like we'll be gathering the sheep stealers!"

Chapter Nine

THE CAPTURE

By ten o'clock that morning the stage was set for the capture of the sheep stealers. Davie and Iain and Piper Rory had joined Father in keeping the watch at Truim Barracks.

"I've found a bonnie spot for us to keep a lookout," said Father, when they arrived. "See up there in the old keep, there's a square room in the stone tower, or at least the floor of it. We can stay up there as cozy as can be and see all that's going on in the Barracks. You can see out to the Great North Road too, and there's a wee window at the back looking off toward Sandy Big Alec's."

"If I'd known what the day's work was to be, I'd have brought a claymore!" said Piper Rory stoutly.

Father shook his head. "We want no trouble! I hope there'll be no need for claymores and the like."

They took the dogs with them up the winding broken stair of the tower. Some of the stones were loose and they had to test each step carefully. It was a fair-sized garrison now, to deal with the sheep stealers—two men and two boys and three dogs.

"I tried to tell Fly to stay at home, but he pleaded with me to come, and I didn't have the heart to turn him back," said Davie.

"He's a plucky dog. He wants to see the thing through!"

Davie covered all the countryside with his telescope. He could pick out sheep on the hill a mile away and more, and it brought Rothiemore clock tower almost into Truim Barracks.

"Och, it's a bonnie glass!" said Piper Rory. "You can almost read the horn markings on yon sheep."

After awhile Davie saw the policemen coming out from Rothiemore on their bicycles, along the Great North Road. "Look now, you can see the dicings on Callum's hat! He's got Geordie Frazer along. . . . "

"Good!" declared Father. "Now we've the law with us, too!"

The two policemen hid themselves in the alder bushes at the head of the lane and dragged their bicycles out of sight. The guards in Truim tower settled themselves down for a long wait.

"I don't expect them until nightfall," said Father, "but there's no telling, now that Fly's run away from Sandy Big Alec!"

After they had eaten their lunch they decided to take turns at the lookouts.

"We'll set up a regular watch, in case we have to keep it all through the night," said Father. "Now Davie you take the place here behind the parapet and cover all the Barracks and the road; and Iain you take the wee window looking off to Sandy Big Alec's. I'll fetch some more water in the jug, and then Rory and I'll have a bit of a nap."

Davie was sleepy too, after being up so early in the morning. He leaned on the broken stone wall of the tower and looked down into the ancient fortress and out across the countryside, scanning the Great North Road with the glass from time to time when cars or trucks went along it. All was quiet and peaceful that afternoon in the broad valley of the Spey.

Davie tried to imagine what it would be like to have been one of Prince Charlie's clansmen hiding out at Truim after the battle of Culloden two hundred years ago—watching over Strath Spey for Cumberland's soldiers. Or what a young English soldier lad would have been thinking about, far away from home up here in the north of Scotland to awe the fierce highland clans after the uprising of 1715. Aye, and there had been other battles too, when clan fought clan—the MacPhersons and the Camerons.

Now, there were battles no longer, but here he was keeping a watch for the sheep stealers . . . . .

"Hist! There's someone coming over the hill" cried Iain. "Give us your glass, Davie! . . . . . . Aye, it's Sandy Big Alec right enough!"

"Certain 't is!" said Piper Rory, in a hoarse whisper. "Coming to look over his plunder. Well he has a surprise waiting for him!"

They all took turns at the telescope, crowding in close to the window slit. Sandy Big Alec came ambling down the brae, with his two dogs, looking all around to the right and left of him as he walked.

"He's keeping a wary eye out," said Rory. "We'll have to be careful now and not make a botch o' it!"

The big man was heading straight for Truim Barracks. He growled at the dogs when they started across the moor, and they fell in at his heels.

"We'll wait until he gets right down by the sheep," Father whispered. "Then we'll rush down and face him with it. Davie, you signal to

Callum and Geordie and then watch with the glass to make sure they've seen!"

Davie turned and hurried across to the parapet. But he didn't signal to the policemen——

"Wait now!" he exclaimed. "There's a car turning in off the road. It's a tourist bus! . . . . . ."

"Bless me, so 't is! Now what . . .?"

"There's no tourists in it," said Davie, following it with the glass. "Just the driver, and another man. Och, it's a rackety old bus!"

"It's not a real tourist bus at all!" whispered Father. "They've planned to meet Sandy Big Alec here at Truim Barracks, and they'll load the sheep into it! It would hold the lot."

"Aye, it would hold the lot, for there's no seats in it!" said Davie, watching the bus coming up the lane.

"Ha! That's it, then!"

"Where's Sandy Big Alec now?"

Iain had been keeping an eye on Sandy Big Alec through the narrow window slit.

"He's stopped!" Iain whispered, and his voice was trembling. "He's seen the bus comin'. Look, he's called in the dogs and he's down in a wee gully!"

"That's queer now!" said Rory. "What would you make of it?"

"We'll just lie quiet here and see" Father said. "Nobody make a move 'til I give the word!"

The dilapidated old bus chugged up the lane and swung around in a wide circle on the grass. Then it backed through a break in the wall, into the empty square in the centre of the Barracks. The two men got out.

"It's the men from the bothy!" whispered Davie. "The same two we saw on Craig Dhu the day Sandy Big Alec came for Fly!"

113

Iain scuttled over from his post at the window slit. "Sandy Big Alec's crept up out of the wee gully and is stealing over to the break in the wall. I can't see him any more."

"Sh! There he is now! You can just see his cap."

The two men talked for a moment beside the bus, while Sandy Big Alec spied on them over the broken wall. Then the smaller man—the one called Harry—climbed up into the bus and backed it over toward the cellar where the sheep were penned. The burly big fellow directed him and finally said "Good enough, Harry!"

That was when Sandy Big Alec jumped out of his hiding place. He ran across the grass, roaring at the two men——

"Hissht, there! What d' you think you're doin' now! You're a pair of thieves and robbers . . . !"

"Sandy Big Alec's *not* the sheep stealer at all!" cried Davie. There was so much noise with Sandy Big Alec's bellowings echoing round in the ruins, that there was no need to whisper any more.

"Come on! Now!" cried Father, and headed the rush down the stone stairs. Davie waited a moment to signal Callum and Geordie, but it wasn't necessary for the two policemen were pedalling furiously up the rough lane on their bicycles.

The men rushed in to help. And not a moment too soon! The clumsy farmer started after the two strangers, waving his stick, but the burly sheep stealer caught the stick and sent it flying, and swung such a punch to Sandy Big Alec's stomach that the poor fellow crumpled to the ground. By then Father and Rory entered the battle, and Iain and Davie caught the smaller man Harry by the legs and by the coat and in a moment they were sprawled in a heap on the ground. The dogs were beside themselves with excitement but they were no help. They could handle sheep, but what were they to do about this tangle of men and boys?

It was a grim fight for awhile. Truim Barracks had been the scene

of many a battle in days gone by. Some of them had been bloodier perhaps, but none more fiercely fought.

The big sheep stealer clouted Piper Rory in the eye and knocked him clear over the poles and in among the sheep. The man Harry was small, but he was mean and tricky. He wrenched himself free from the boys and started for the bus, but the dogs were in his way. He tripped over Fly, and Fly forgot all his training for a moment and bit the man's ankle. Och, how he yelled and swore! In a moment Davie was on top of him, and Iain clung to his legs for dear life. When Davie looked around he saw that, somehow or other, Father was getting the best of the burly thief, and the tide of victory was strong in their favour.

By the time Callum Campbell and Geordie Frazer leaped off their bicycles, the capture of the sheep stealers was complete. They saw they were beaten, and there was no chance of escape. The smaller man just sat there on the ground looking glum, while Geordie Frazer put the handcuffs on him.

"It was brawly done," said Callum Campbell. "We couldn't have managed it any better ourselves!"

"Aye, and not near as well maybe!" grinned Piper Rory. His eye was red and swollen.

They put the sheep stealers onto the bus and shoved their bicycles into it too and Geordie got behind the wheel. Callum Campbell took off his diced cap and wiped the sweat from his forehead with a big red handkerchief.

"Well, that's that!" he said.

When the bus had rumbled off down the lane with its load of policemen and sheep stealers and bicycles, Piper Rory said, "Well now that was a crafty bit o' work!—having a tour bus to carry away stolen sheep. It wouldn't be noticed on the roads, and they could drive right through to Glasgow and beyond."

Sandy Big Alec looked flustered and uneasy. "Well you've saved my sheep, and y' saved me from a beating. It would have gone hard with me if you hadn't been here." It was not easy for Sandy Big Alec to say what was on his mind.

"Och, I guess I'm not a very good neighbour to any man! I've been thinkin' it isn't much of a life if all you've got is money in the bank and a hirsel full of fine sheep, and nobody to speak well of you at all."

"Ah now, Mr. MacMurchie, it isn't like that, quite!" said Father. "We're right glad to catch the thieves at last—though in all honesty I must admit I thought you had a hand in it when Fly came home this morning with a bruise on his back."

"It's not from *my* stick, that bruise!" Sandy Big Alec said quickly. "Fly wouldn't eat his supper yester evening, and went off in the night."

"Yes, yes, it was the sheep stealers that gave him the whack. He must have come on them when he was crossing Craig Dhu, and tried to bring our Crubenbeg sheep down the hill. Aye, and he *did* too! He brought thirty of them down to us this morning."

"Aye, Fly belongs with you at Crubenbeg Farm! I've known it all along. David, he's your dog now, like he's always been—even though it was my money that bought him from the old tramp."

Davie's heart stopped for a second, and then hammered along like an engine. Fly was *his* dog! Fly was *his* dog, and going to stay for good and all at Crubenbeg!

"There's some things money won't buy," said Father quietly. Davie knelt down beside the wee dog and hugged him close, and Fly licked a dozen kisses on his cheek.

"Aye, there's things money won't buy, right enough," said Sandy Big Alec. He took out his handkerchief and blew his nose loudly. "Well, I must be getting on home . . . but if you're needin' a hand with your gathering any time I'd be obliged if you'd come over and ask me to help!"

"Aye, we'll just do that now, won't we, Rory?"

"Sure . . . aye . . . aye, certain we will!" stammered Piper Rory, scratching his head to try and understand this miracle.

"And thanks for letting us keep the wee dog, sir!" said Davie.

"Och, don't say anything at all. He belongs with you!" and Sandy Big Alec stamped off across the moor toward Craig Dhu.

They watched him until he crossed the burn.

"Well I *never!*" exclaimed Piper Rory.

"I think, maybe, we've done more today than catch the sheep stealers," said Father.

Davie knelt there on the grass holding the dog tight. "Ah Fly, Fly! You're my own dog," he whispered. "You'll be a grand dog for the hill—and maybe we'll have a fling at the Trials again next year, the two of us!"

Then a strange thing happened! There came the sound of singing, just beyond the fortress wall——

"Charlie, ye are welcome, welcome, welcome.
    Charlie ye are welcome, to Scotland and to me!
"The clans are all agatherin', agatherin', agatherin'.
    The clans are all agatherin', to set their country free!
"The swords they are all ready, ready, ready.
    The swords they are all ready, and Cumberland will flee!
"The colours they are flyin', flyin', fl . . . . "

There at the break in the wall appeared old Billy! Old Billy Bayne! As large as life, and as ragged as ever!

The song died away on the lips of the tattered old man as he caught sight of the visitors in Truim Barracks. He blinked for a moment as if wondering whether they were real or whether they were some of the ghosts of Truim from the troubled past.

"Are ye . . . are ye for Bonnie Prince Charlie?" he asked in a

quavering voice. Then he shook his head and swished his stick through the air, and said, "Och no! That was all long since, wasn't it now?"

Father spoke up. "You're well again, Mr. Bayne. We were wondering . . . . ."

"Och, aye! Hail and hearty! And sound o' lung and limb! Old Billy Bayne's made of stern stuff. I was comin' by and thought I'd look in at Truim and pay my respects to my bonnie Prince and the poor lads who stood by him in the '45."

"You've helped us catch the sheep stealers. Davie here remembered you'd said to keep an eye on Truim Barracks!"

"Here's the wee dog" said Davie, pushing Fly out in front. "D'you remember Fly, that you sold to Sandy Big Alec?"

Billy Bayne pulled at his whiskers. "Aye. He's come to be a fine dog, eh? He's from Old Hemp ye know, like I said. I'm glad ye have him— he took a fancy to ye from the first . . . Would ye have a penny for a poor old singer, any one of ye?"

"To be sure we've a penny, and more!" Father declared. "You'll have one of the biggest suppers you ever ate . . . and a bed too, at Cruben-beg!"

Old Billy shrugged. "I'll take the supper, and thank ye. But no' the bed . . . If ye don't mind, I'll sleep the night in Prince Charlie's Cave, where my bonnie lord lay down his troubled head many a long year ago."

"Take him over then, Davie, you and Iain, while Rory and I look after the sorting of yon sheep. We'll drive Sandy Big Alec's onto his hill on the way, and put our own in the fold."

"Come on then, sir!" said Davie. "Come along, Fly, and we'll show Mr. Bayne what a likely dog you've turned out!"

So they set out over the slopes of Craig Dhu, with old Billy lustily singing his trollolays about Prince Charlie and Scottish battles long ago. The September sun was warm and mellow over the highlands, and all seemed right with the world at last. The sheep stealers wouldn't be bothering them any more, and Davie had a fine glass and a dog of his own—a grand dog for the hill!